Selena felt... ...sed.

All of her secrets. All of herself.

"So that's it?" he asked. "We kiss after all these years of friendship, and you're fine."

"Knox," she said, "you don't want me to be anything but fine. Believe me. It's better for the two of us if we just move on like nothing happened. I don't think either of us needs this right now." *Or ever.*

She wanted to hide. But she knew that if she did hide it would only let him know how close he was delving into things she didn't want him anywhere near. Things she didn't want anyone near.

"Yeah," he said. "I guess so."

"You don't want to talk about our feelings, do you?" she asked, knowing that she sounded testy.

"Absolutely not. I've had enough feelings for a lifetime."

"I'm right there with you. I don't have any interest in messing up a good friendship over a little bit of sex."

Knox walked past her, moving back into the shop. Then he paused, kicking his head back out of the doorway. "I agree with you, Selena, except for one little thing. With me, there wouldn't be anything little about the sex."

The Rancher's Baby is part of Texas Cattleman's Club: The Impostor series—Will the scandal of the century lead to love for these rich ranchers?

Dear Reader,

When I was asked to take part in the legendary Texas Cattleman's Club series for Harlequin Desire, I was thrilled. It's an honor to be able to take part in such a well-beloved series.

The Rancher's Baby is about two friends, Knox and Selena, who end up with a very permanent consequence when their long-buried attraction ignites. Writing about friends becoming more is one of my favorite things, but this story also has one of my other favorite themes.

How brave it is to choose to love, even when you've been hurt.

Of all my heroes, Knox has definitely experienced one of the most devastating losses I can think of. And for him, choosing to love when he knows how much love can cost is much more terrifying than anything else on earth.

But if anyone is worth it, it's Selena.

I hope you enjoy my contribution to this series.

Happy reading!

Maisey

MAISEY YATES

THE RANCHER'S BABY

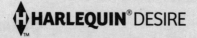

Special thanks and acknowledgment are given
to Maisey Yates for her contribution to the Texas
Cattleman's Club: The Impostor miniseries.

ISBN-13: 978-1-335-97123-4

The Rancher's Baby

Copyright © 2018 by Harlequin Books S.A.

Recycling programs
for this product may
not exist in your area.

Printed in U.S.A.   www.Harlequin.com

Maisey Yates is a *New York Times* bestselling author of more than thirty romance novels. She has a coffee habit she has no interest in kicking, and a slight Pinterest addiction. She lives with her husband and children in the Pacific Northwest. When Maisey isn't writing she can be found singing in the grocery store, shopping for shoes online and probably not doing dishes. Check out her website: maiseyyates.com.

Books by Maisey Yates

Harlequin Desire

Copper Ridge

Take Me, Cowboy
Hold Me, Cowboy
Seduce Me, Cowboy

Texas Cattleman's Club: The Impostor

The Rancher's Baby

HQN Books

Copper Ridge

Shoulda Been a Cowboy
Part Time Cowboy
Brokedown Cowboy
Bad News Cowboy
A Copper Ridge Christmas
One Night Charmer

Visit her Author Profile page on Harlequin.com, or maiseyyates.com, for more titles!

One

My fake ex-husband died at sea and all I got was this stupid letter.

That was Selena Jacobs's very dark thought as she stood in the oppressive funeral home clutching said letter so tightly she was wearing a thumbprint into the envelope.

She supposed that her initial thought wasn't true—strictly speaking. The letter proclaimed she was the heir to Will's vast estate.

It was just that there were four other women at the funeral who had been promised the exact same thing. And Selena couldn't fathom why Will would have made her the beneficiary of anything, except maybe that hideous bearskin rug he'd gotten from his grandfather that he'd had in his dorm at school. The one she'd hated because the sightless glass eyes had creeped her out.

Yeah, that she would have believed Will had left her.

His entire estate, not so much.

But then, she was still having trouble believing Will was dead. It seemed impossible. He had always been so...so *much*. Of everything. So much energy. So much light. So much of a pain in the ass sometimes. It seemed impossible that a solemn little urn could contain everything Will Sanders had been. And yet there it was.

Though she supposed that Will wasn't entirely contained in the urn. Will, and the general fallout of his life—good and bad—was contained here in this room.

There were...well, there were a lot of women standing around looking bereft, each one of them holding letters identical to hers. Their feelings on the contents of the letters were different than hers. They must be. They didn't all run multimillion-dollar corporations.

Selena's muted reaction to her supposed inheritance was in some part due to the fact that she doubted the authenticity of the letter. But the other part was because she simply didn't need the money. Not at this point in her life.

These other women...

Well, she didn't really know. One of them was holding a chubby toddler, her expression blank. There was another in a sedate dress that flowed gently over what looked to be a burgeoning baby bump. Will had been too charming for his own good, it seemed.

Selena shuddered.

She didn't know the nature of those women's relationships to Will, but she had her suspicions. And the very idea of being left in a similar situation made her skin crawl.

There were reasons she kept men at arm's length. The vulnerability of being left pregnant was one of them. A very compelling one.

As for the other reasons? Well, every woman in this room was a living, breathing affirmation of Selena's life choices.

Heartbroken wives, ex-wives and baby mamas.

Selena might technically be an ex-wife, but she wasn't one in the traditional sense. And she wasn't heartbroken. She was hurt. She was grieving. And she was full of regret. She wished more than anything that she and Will had patched up their friendship.

But, of course, she had imagined that there was plenty of time to revive a friendship they'd left behind in college.

There hadn't been plenty of time. Will didn't have any more time.

Grief clutched at her heart and she swallowed hard, turning away from the urn to face the entry door at the back of the room.

The next visitor to walk in made her already battered heart jolt with shocked recognition.

Knox McCoy.

She really hadn't expected him to come. He had been pretty scarce for the past couple of years, and she honestly couldn't blame him. When he had texted her the other day, he'd said he wouldn't be attending the funeral, and he hadn't needed to say why.

She suspected he hadn't been to one since the one for his daughter, Eleanor.

She tried to quell the nerves fluttering in her stomach as Knox walked deeper into the room, his gray eyes locking with hers. She had known the man for more than a decade. She had made her decisions regarding him, and he...

Well, he had never felt the way about her that she did about him.

He looked as gorgeous as ever. His broad shoulders, chest and trim waist outlined perfectly in the gray custom-made suit with matching charcoal tie. His brown hair was pushed back off his forehead, longer than he used to keep it. He was also sporting a beard, which was not typical of him. He had deep grooves between his dark brows, lines worn into his handsome face by the pain of the past few years.

She wanted to go to him. She wanted to press her thumb right there at those worry lines and smooth them out. Just the thought of touching him made her feel restless. Hot.

And really, really, she needed not to be having a full-blown Knox episode at her ex-husband's funeral.

Regardless of the real nature of her relationship with Will, her reaction to Knox was inappropriate. Beyond inappropriate.

"How are you doing?" he asked, his expression full of concern.

When he made that face his eyebrows locked together and the grooves deepened.

"Oh, I've been better," she said honestly.

A lopsided smile curved the corner of his mouth upward and he reached out, his thumb brushing over her cheek. His skin was rough, his hands those of a rancher. A working man. His wealth came from the chain of upscale grocery stores he owned, but his passion was in working the land at his ranch in Wyoming.

Her gaze met his, and the blank sadness she saw in his eyes made her stomach feel hollow.

She wondered if the ranch still held his passion. She wondered if anything did anymore.

"Me, too," he said, his voice rough.

"Will is such an inconsiderate ass," she said, her voice trembling. "Leave it to him to go and die like this."

"Yeah," Knox agreed. "His timing is pretty terrible. Plus, you know he just wanted the attention."

She laughed, and as the laugh escaped her lips, a tear slid down her cheek.

She'd met Knox at Harvard. From completely different backgrounds—his small-town Texan childhood worlds away from her high-society East Coast life—they had bonded quickly. And then... Then her grandfather had died, which had ripped her heart square out of her chest. He had been the only person in her family who had ever loved her. Who had ever instilled hope in her for the future.

And with his death had come the trust fund. A trust fund she could only access when she was twenty-five. Or married.

The idea of asking Knox to marry her had been... Well, it had been unthinkable. For a whole host of reasons. She hadn't wanted to get married, not for real. And her feelings for Knox had been real. Or at least, she had known perfectly well they were on the verge of being real, and she'd needed desperately for them to stay manageable. For him to stay a friend.

Then their friend Will had seen her crying one afternoon and she'd explained everything. He had offered himself as her solution. She hadn't been in a position to say no.

Control of her money had provided freedom from her father. It had given her the ability to complete her education on her own terms. It had also ended up ruining her friendship with Will. In the meantime, Knox had met someone else. Someone he eventually married.

She blinked, bringing herself firmly back to the present. There was no point thinking about all of that. She didn't. Not often. Her friendship with Knox had survived college, and they had remained close in spite of the fact that they were both busy with their respective careers.

It was Will. Whenever Will was added to the mix she couldn't help but think of those years. Of that one stupid, reckless decision that had ended up doing a lot of damage in the end.

For some reason, she suddenly felt hollow and weak. She wobbled slightly, and Knox reached toward her as if he would touch her again. She wasn't sure that would be as fortifying as he thought it might be.

But then the doors to the funeral home opened again and she looked up at the same time Knox looked over his shoulder.

And the world stopped.

Because the person who walked through the door was the person who was meant to be in that urn.

It was Will Sanders, and he was very much alive.

Then the world really did start to spin, and Selena didn't know how to stand upright in it.

That was how she found herself crashing to the floor, and then everything was dark.

Fucking Will. Of course he wasn't actually dead.

That was Knox's prevailing thought as he dropped to his knees, wrapping his arm around Selena and pulling her into his lap.

No one was paying attention to one passed-out woman, because they were a hell of a lot more concerned with the walking corpse who had just appeared at his own funeral.

It was clear Will was just as shocked as everyone else.

Except for maybe Selena.

Had she loved the bastard that much? It had been more than ten years since Will and Selena had been married, and Selena rarely talked about Will, but Knox supposed he should know as well as anyone that sometimes not talking about something indicated you thought about it a whole hell of a lot.

That it mattered much more than the things that rolled off your tongue with routine frequency.

As he watched the entire room erupt in shock, Knox was filled with one dark thought.

At the last funeral he had attended he would have given everything he owned for the little body in the casket to come walking into the room. Would've given anything to wake up and find it all a nightmare.

He would have even traded places with his daughter. Would have buried himself six feet down if it would have meant Eleanor would come back.

But of course that hadn't happened. He was living a fucking soap opera at the wrong damned moment.

He looked down at Selena's gray face and cupped her cheek, patting it slightly, doing his best to revive her. He didn't know what you were supposed to do when a woman fainted. And God knew caregiving was not his strong suit.

His ex-wife would be the first to testify to that.

Selena's skin felt clammy, a light sweat beading on her brow. He wasn't used to seeing his tough-as-nails friend anything but self-assured. Even when things were terrible, she usually did what she had done only a few moments ago. She made a joke. She stood strong.

When Eleanor had died Selena had stood with him until he couldn't stand, and then she had sat with him. She had been there for him through all of that.

Apparently, ex-husbands returning from the beyond were her breaking point.

"Come on, Selena," he murmured, brushing some of her black hair out of her face. "You can wake up now. You've done a damn decent job of stealing his thunder. Anything else is just showing off at this point."

Her sooty eyelashes fluttered, and her eyes opened, her whiskey-colored gaze foggy. "What happened?"

He looked around the room, at the commotion stirring around them. "It seems Will has come back from the dead."

Two

Will wasn't dead.

Selena kept playing that thought over and over in her mind as Knox drove them down the highway.

She wasn't entirely clear on what had happened to her car, or why Knox was driving her. Or what she was going to do with her car later. She had been too consumed with putting one foot in front of the other while Knox led her from the funeral home, safely ensconced her in his rental car and began to take them… Well, she didn't know where.

She slid her hand around the back of her neck, beneath her hair, her skin damp and hot against her palm. She felt awful. She felt... Well, like she had passed out on the floor of a funeral home.

"Where are we going?" she asked.

"To your place."

"You don't know where I live," she mumbled, her lips numb.

"I do."

"No, you don't, Knox. I've moved since the last time you came to visit."

"I looked you up."

Knox hadn't come back to Royal since his divorce. She couldn't blame him. There was a lot of bad wrapped up in Royal for him. Seeing as this was where he'd lived with his family most of the year when he'd been married.

"I'm not listed." She attempted to make the words sound crisp.

"You know me better than that, honey," he said, that slow Texas drawl winding itself through her veins and turning her blood into fire. "I don't need a phone book to find someone."

"Obviously, Knox. No one has used a phone book since 2004. But I meant it's not like you can just look up my address on the internet."

"Figure of speech, Selena. Also, I have connections. Resources."

She made a disgusted sound and pressed her forehead against the window. It wasn't cold enough.

"You sent me a Christmas card," he said, his tone

maddeningly steady. "I added your address to my contacts."

"Well," she said. "Damn my manners. Apparently they've made me traceable."

"Not very stealthy."

"*And* you're rude," she said, ignoring him. "Because you did not send me a Christmas card back."

"I had my secretary send you something."

"What did she send me?" Selena asked.

"It was either a gold watch or a glass owl figurine," he said.

"What did she do, send you links to two different things, and then you said choose either one?"

"Yes."

"That doesn't count as a present, Knox. And it certainly doesn't equal my very personal Christmas card."

"You didn't have an assistant send the card?" he asked, sounding incredulous.

"I did not. I addressed it myself, painstakingly by hand while I was eating a TV dinner."

"A TV dinner?" he asked, chuckling. "That doesn't jibe with your healthy-lifestyle persona."

"It was a frozen dinner from Green Fair Pantry," she said pointedly, mentioning the organic fair-trade grocery-store chain Knox owned. "If those aren't healthy, then you have some explaining to do yourself."

She was starting to feel a little bit more human,

but along with that feeling came a dawning realization of the enormity of everything that had just happened.

"Will is alive," she said, just to confirm.

"It looks that way," Knox said, tightening his hold on the steering wheel. She did her best not to watch the way the muscles in his forearms shifted, did her best to ignore just how large his hands looked, how large *he* looked in this car that was clearly too small for him. One that he would never have driven in his real life.

Knox was much more of a pickup truck kind of man, no matter how much money he made. Little luxury vehicles were not his thing.

"I guess I don't get his bearskin rug, then," she said absently.

"What?"

"Don't you remember that appalling thing he used to have in his dorm room?"

Knox shot her a look out of the corner of his eye. "Not really. Hey, are you okay?"

"I am… I don't know. I mean, I guess I'm better than I was when I thought he was ashes in a jar." She cleared her throat. "I'm sorry. Are you okay, Knox? I realize this is probably the first—"

"I don't want to talk about that," he said, cutting her off. "We don't need to. I'm fine."

She didn't think he was. Her throat tightened,

feeling scratchy. "Okay. Anyway, I'm fine, too. My relationship with Will… You know."

Except he didn't. Nobody did. Everyone *thought* they did, but everyone was wrong. Unless, of course, Will had ever talked to anyone about the truth of their marriage, but somehow she doubted it.

"How long had it been since you two had spoken?" Knox asked.

"A long damn time. I don't believe all the things Rich said to me before the divorce. Not anymore. He was toxic."

As little as she tried to think about her short, convenient marriage to Will and what had resulted after, she tried to think about Will's friend Rich Lowell even less. Though she had heard through that reliable Royal grapevine that he and Will had remained friends. It made her wonder why Rich wasn't here.

Rich had been part of their group of friends, though he had always been somewhat on the periphery, and he had been…strange, as far as Selena was concerned. He had liked Will, so much that it had been concerning. And when Will had married Selena, Rich's interest had wandered onto her.

He had never done anything terribly inappropriate, but the increased attention from him had made her uneasy.

But then… Well, he had been in their apartment one night when she'd gotten home from class. He'd produced evidence that Will was after her trust fund—the trust fund that had led to their marriage in the first place. And she needed that money. She needed it so she would never be at her father's mercy again. The trust fund had been everything to her, and Will had said he was marrying her just to help her. She'd trusted him.

Rich had been full of some weird, intense energy Selena hadn't been able to place at the time. Now that she had some distance and a more adult understanding, she felt like maybe Rich had been attracted to her. But more than a simple attraction… he'd been obsessed with Will. It almost seemed, in hindsight, as if he'd been attracted to her *because* he thought Will had her.

And what Rich had said that night… Well, it had just been a lot easier to believe than Will's claim that he wanted to help her because they were friends. Trust had never been easy for her. Will was kind, and that was something she'd wanted. Not because she was attracted to him, but because she had genuinely wanted him to be a real friend. After a life of being thoroughly mistreated by her father, hoping for true friendship was scary.

Selena had spent most of her childhood bracing herself for the punch. Whether emotional or physical. It was much easier to believe she was being tricked than to believe Will was everything he appeared to be.

She and Will had fought. And then they had barely

limped to the finish line of the marriage. They'd waited until the money was in her account, and then they'd divorced.

And their friendship had never been the same.

She had never apologized to him. Grief and regret stabbed her before she remembered—Will wasn't actually dead.

That means you can apologize to him. It means you can fix your friendship.

She needed to. The woman she was now would never have jumped to a conclusion like that, at least not without trying to get to the bottom of it.

But back then, Selena had been half-feral. Honed into a sharp, mean creature from years of being in survival mode.

The way Knox had stuck by her all these years, the kind of friendship he had demonstrated… It had been a huge part of her learning to trust. Learning to believe men could actually be good.

Her ability to trust hadn't changed her stance on love and marriage. And she fought against any encroaching thoughts that conflicted with that stance.

It didn't really matter that Knox sometimes made her think differently about love and marriage. He had married someone else. And she had married someone else. She had married someone else first, in point of fact. It was just that…

It didn't matter.

"I know this dredges up a lot of ancient history,"

Knox said, turning the car off the highway and onto the narrow two-lane road that would take them out to her new cabin. Now that she had the freedom to work remotely most of the time—her skin-care company was so successful she'd hired other people to do the parts that consumed too much time—she had decided to get outside city limits.

Had decided it was time for her to actually make herself a home, instead of living in a holding pattern. Existing solely to build her empire, to increase her net worth.

Nothing had ever felt like home until this place. Everything after college had just been temporary. Before that, it had been a war zone.

This cabin was her refuge. And it was *hers*.

Nestled in the woods, surrounded by sweetgrass and trees, and a river running next to her front porch.

Of course, it wasn't quite as grand as Knox's spread in Jackson Hole, but then, very few places were.

Besides, grandness wasn't the point. This cabin wasn't for show. Wasn't to impress anyone else. It was just to make her happy. And few things in her life had existed for that reason up to this point.

Having achieved some happiness made her long for other things, though. Things she was mostly inured against—like wanting someone to share her life with.

She gritted her teeth, looking resolutely away from Knox as that thought invaded her brain.

"Which is now a little bit annoying," she pointed out. "He's not even dead, and I had to go through all that grief, plus, you know…"

"Thinking about your marriage?"

She snapped her mouth shut, debating how to respond. It was true enough. She had been thinking a lot about her marriage. Not that it had been an actual, physical marriage. More like roommates with official paperwork. "Yes," she said finally.

"Divorce is hell," he said, his voice turning to gravel. "Believe me. I know."

Guilt twisted her stomach. He thought they shared this common bond. The loss of a marriage. In reality, their situations weren't even close to being the same.

"Will and I were only married for a year," she commented. "It's not really the same as you and Cassandra. The two of you were together for twelve years and…"

"I told you, I don't want to talk about it."

Blessedly, distraction came in the form of the left turn that took them off the paved road and onto the gravel road that took them to her cabin.

"Why don't you get this paved?" he asked.

"I like it," she said.

"Why?"

That was a complicated question, with a complicated answer. But he was her friend and she was glad to be off the topic of marriages, so she figured she would take a stab at it. "Because it's nothing like the driveway that we had when I was growing up. Which was smooth and paved and circular, and led up to the most ridiculous brick monstrosity."

"So this is like inverse nostalgia?"

"Yes."

He lifted a shoulder. "I understand that better than you might think."

He pulled up to the front of the cabin and she stayed resolutely in her seat until he rounded to her side and opened the door for her. Then she blinked, looking up into the sun, at the way his broad shoulders blotted it out. "What about my car?" she asked.

"I'm going to have someone bring it. Don't worry."

"I could go get it," she said.

"I have a feeling it's best if you lie low for a little bit."

"Why would I do that?"

"Well," he said. "Your ex-husband just came back from the dead, and both of you cause quite a bit of media interest. You were named as beneficiary of his estate along with four other women, and that's a lot of money."

"But Will isn't dead, and I don't care about his money. I have my own."

"Very few people are going to believe that, Selena,"

Knox said, his tone grave. "Most people don't acknowledge the concept of having enough money. They only understand wanting more."

"What are you saying? That I'm…in danger?"

"I don't know. But we don't know what's going on with Will, and you were brought into this. You're a target, for all we know. Someone is in an urn, and you have a letter that brought you here."

"You're jumping to conclusions, Knox."

"Maybe," he said, "but I swear to God, Selena, I'd rather have you safe than end up in an urn. That I couldn't deal with."

She looked at the deep intensity in his expression. "I'll be safe."

"You need to lie low for a while."

"What does that mean? What am I supposed to do?"

Knox shrugged, the casual gesture at odds with the steely determination in his gray eyes. "I figured I would keep you company."

Three

Selena looked less than thrilled by the prospect of sticking close to home while the situation with Will got sorted out.

Knox didn't particularly care whether or not Selena was thrilled. He wanted her safe. As far as he was concerned, this was some shady shit, and until it was resolved, he didn't want any of it getting near her.

All of it was weird. The five women who had been presented with nearly identical letters telling them that they had inherited Will's estate, and then Will not actually being dead. The fact that someone else had been living Will's life.

Maybe none of it would touch Selena. But there was nothing half so pressing in Knox's life as his best friend's safety.

His business did not require him to micromanage it. That was the perk of making billions, as far as he was concerned. You didn't have to be in an office all the damned time if it didn't suit you.

Plus, it was all…pointless.

He shook off the hollow feeling of his chest caving in on itself and turned his focus back to Selena.

"I don't need you to stay here with me," she said, all but scampering across the lawn and to her porch.

"I need to stay here with you," he returned. He was more than happy to make it about him. Because he knew she wouldn't be able to resist. She was worried about him. She didn't need to be. But she was. And if he played into that, then she would give him whatever he wanted.

"But it's a waste of your time," she pointed out, digging in her purse for her keys, pulling them out and jamming one of them in the lock.

"Maybe," he said. "But I swear to God, Selena, if I have to go to a funeral with a big picture of *you* up at the front of the room…"

"No one has threatened me," she said, turning the key and pushing the door open.

"And I'd rather not wait and see if someone does."

"You're being hypervigilant," she returned.

"Yes," he said. "I am." He gritted his teeth. "Some

things you can't control, Selena. Some bad stuff you can't stop. But I'm not going to decide everything is fine here and risk losing you just because I went home earlier than I should have."

She looked up at him, the stubborn light in her eyes fading. "Okay. If you need to do this, that's fine."

Selena walked into the front entrance of the cabin and threw her purse down on an entryway table. Typical Selena. There was a hook right above the table, but she didn't hang the purse up. No. That extra step would be considered a waste of time in her estimation. Never mind that her disorganization often meant she spent extra time looking for things.

He looked around the spacious, bright room. It was clean. Surprisingly so.

"This place is… It's nice. Spotless."

"I have a housekeeper," she said, turning to face him, crossing her arms beneath her breasts and offering up a lopsided smile.

For a moment, just a moment, his eyes dipped down to examine those breasts. His gut tightened and he resolutely turned his focus back to her eyes. Selena was a woman. He had known that for a long time. But she wasn't a woman whose breasts concerned him. She never had been.

When they had met in college he had thought she was beautiful, sure. A man would have to be blind not to see that. But she had also been brittle. Skittish and damaged. And it had taken work on his part to forge a friendship with her.

Once he had become her friend, he had never wanted to do anything to compromise that bond. And if he had been a little jealous of Will Sanders somehow convincing her that marriage was worth the risk, Knox had never indulged that jealousy.

Then Will had hurt her, devastated her, divorced her. And after that, Selena had made her feelings about relationships pretty clear. Anyway, at that point, he had been serious about Cassandra, and then they had gotten married.

His friendship with Selena outlasted both of their marriages, and had proved that the decision he'd made back in college, to not examine her breasts, had been a solid one.

One he was going to hold to.

"Well, thank God for the housekeeper," he said, his tone dry. "Living all the way out here by yourself, if you didn't have someone taking care of you you'd be liable to die beneath a pile of your own clothes."

She huffed. "You don't know me, Knox."

"Oh, honey," he said, "I do."

A long, slow moment stretched between them and her olive skin was suddenly suffused with color. It probably wasn't nice of him to tease her about her propensity toward messiness. "Well," she said, her tone stiff. "I do have a guest room. And I suppose it would be unkind of me to send you packing back to Wyoming on your first night here in Royal."

"Downright mean," he said, schooling his expression into one of pure innocence. As much as he could manage.

It occurred to him then that the two of them hadn't really spent much time together in the past couple of years. And they hadn't spent time alone together in the past decade. He had been married to another woman, and even though his friendship with Selena had been platonic, and Cassandra had never expressed any jealousy toward her, it would have been stretching things a bit for him to spend the night at her place with no one else around.

"Well," she said, tossing her glossy black hair over her shoulder. "I am a little mean."

"Are you?"

She smiled broadly, the expression somewhere between a grin and a snarl. "It has been said."

"By who?" he asked, feeling instantly protective of her. She had always brought that out in him. Even though now it felt like a joke, that he could feel protective of anyone. He hadn't managed to protect the most important people in his life.

"I wasn't thinking of a particular incident," she responded, wandering toward the kitchen, kicking her shoes off as she went, leaving them right where she stepped out of them, like fuchsia afterthoughts.

"Did Will say you were mean?"

She turned to face him, cocking one dark brow. "Will didn't have strong feelings for me one way or the other, Knox. Certainly not in the time since the divorce." She began to bustle around the kitchen, and he leaned against the island, placing his hand on the high-gloss marble countertop, watching as she worked with efficiency, getting mugs and heating water. She was making tea, and she wasn't even asking him if he wanted any. She would simply present him with some. And he wouldn't drink it, because he didn't like tea.

A pretty familiar routine for the two of them.

"He put you pretty firmly off of marriage," Knox pointed out, "so I would say he's also not completely blameless."

"You're not supposed to speak ill of the dead. Or the undead, in Will's case."

He drummed his fingers on the counter. "You know, that does present an interesting question."

"What question is that?"

"Who died?" he asked.

"What do you mean?"

"There were ashes in that urn. Obviously they weren't Will's. But if he's not dead, then who is?"

Selena frowned. "Maybe no one's dead. Maybe it's ashes from a campfire."

"Why would someone go to all that trouble? Why would somebody go to that much trouble to fake Will's death? Or to fake anyone's death? Again, I think this has something to do with those letters. With all of the women in his life being made beneficiaries of his estate. And this is why I'm not leaving you here by yourself."

"Because you're a high-handed, difficult, surly, obnoxious…"

"Are you finished?"

"Just a second," she said, taking her kettle off the stove and pouring hot water into two of the mugs on the counter. "Irritating, overbearing…"

"Wealthy, handsome, incredibly generous."

"Yes, it's true," she said. "But I prefer beautiful to handsome. I mean, I assume you were offering up descriptions of me."

She shoved a mug in his direction, smiling brilliantly. He did not tell her he didn't want any. He did not remind her that he had told her at least fifteen times over the years that he did not drink tea. Instead, he curled his fingers around the mug and pulled it close, knowing she wouldn't realize he wasn't having any.

It was just one of her charming quirks. The fact that she could be totally oblivious to what was happening around her. Cast-off shoes in the middle of her floor were symptoms of it. It wasn't that Selena was an airhead; she was incredibly insightful, actually. It was just that her head seemed to continually be full of thoughts about what was next. Sometimes, all that thinking made it hard to keep her rooted in the present.

She rested her elbows on the counter, then placed her chin in her palms, looking suddenly much younger than she had only a moment ago. Reminding him of the girl he had known in college.

And along with that memory came an old urge. To reach out, to brush her hair out of her face, to trace the line of her lower lip with the edge of his thumb. To take a chance with all of her spiky indignation and press his mouth against hers.

Instead, he lifted his mug to his lips and took a long drink, the hot water and bitterly acidic tea burning his throat as he swallowed.

He really, really didn't like tea.

"You know," she said, tapping the side of her mug, straightening. "I do have a few projects you could work on around here. If you're going to stay with me."

"You're putting me to work?"

"Yes. If you're going to stay with me, you need to earn your keep."

"I'm earning my keep by guarding you."

"From a threat you don't even know exists."

"I know a few things," he said, holding up his hand and counting off each thing with his fingers. "I know someone is dead. I know you are mysteriously named as a beneficiary of a lot of money, as are a bunch of other women."

"And one assumes that we are no longer going to inherit any money since Will isn't dead."

"But someone wanted us all to think that he was. Hell, maybe somebody wanted him to be dead."

"Are you a private detective now? The high-end health-food grocery-chain business not working out for you?"

"It's working out for me very well, actually. Which you know. And don't change the subject."

A smile tugged at the corner of her mouth.

He was genuinely concerned about her well-being; he wasn't making that up. But there was something else, too. Something holding him here. Or maybe it was just something keeping him from going back to Wyoming. He had avoided Royal, and Texas altogether, since his divorce. Had avoided going anywhere that reminded him of his former life. He'd owned the ranch in Jackson Hole for over a decade, but he, Cassandra and Eleanor hadn't spent as much time there as they had here.

Still, for some reason, now that he was back, the idea of returning to that gigantic ranch house in Wyoming to rattle around all by himself didn't seem appealing.

There was a reason he had gotten married. A reason he and Cassandra had started a family. It was what he had wanted. An answer to his lifetime of loneliness. To the deficit he had grown up with. He had wanted everything. A wife, children, money.

All of those things that would keep him from feeling like he had back then.

But he had learned the hard way that children could be taken from you. That marriages crumbled. And that money didn't mean a damn thing in the end.

If he'd had a choice, if the universe would have asked him, he would have given up the money first.

Of course, he hadn't realized that until it was too late.

Not that there was any fixing it. Not that there had been a choice. Cancer didn't care if you were a billionaire.

It didn't care if a little girl was your entire world.

Now all he had was a big empty house. One that currently had an invitation to a charity event on the fridge. An invitation he just couldn't deal with right now.

He looked back up at Selena. Yeah, staying here for a few days was definitely more appealing than heading straight back to Jackson Hole.

"Okay," he said. "What projects did you have in mind?"

He never said he didn't like tea.

That was Selena's first thought when she got up the next morning and set about making coffee for Knox and herself. Selena found it singularly odd that he never refused the tea. She served it to him sometimes just to see if he would. But he never did. He just sat there holding it. Which was funny, because Knox was not a passive man. Far from it.

In fact, in college, he had been her role model for that reason. He was authoritative. He asked for what he wanted. He went for what he wanted. And Selena had wanted to remake herself in his mold. She'd found him endlessly fascinating.

Though she had to admit, as she bustled around the kitchen, he was just as fascinating now. But now she had a much firmer grasp on what she wanted. On what was possible.

She had felt a little weird about him staying with her at first, which was old baggage creeping in. Old feelings. That crush she'd had on him in college that had never had a hope in hell of going anywhere. Not because she thought it was impossible for him to de- sire her, but because she knew there was no future in it. And she needed Knox as a friend much more than she needed him as a…well…the alternative.

But then last night, as they had been standing in the kitchen, she had looked at him. Really looked at him. Those lines between his brows were so deep, and his eyes were so incredibly…changed. Physi- cally, she supposed he kind of looked the same, and yet he didn't. He was reduced. And it was a ter- rible thing to see a man like him reduced. But she couldn't blame him.

What happened with Eleanor had been such a shock. Such a horrible, hideous shock.

One day, she had been a normal, healthy toddler, and then she had been lethargic. Right after that came the cancer diagnosis, and in only a couple of months she was gone.

The entire situation had been surreal and heart-breaking. For her. And Eleanor wasn't even her child. But her friend's pain had been so real, so raw... She had no idea how he had coped with it, and now she could see that he hadn't really. That he still was trying to cope.

He hadn't come back to Texas since Eleanor's death, and she had seen him only a couple of times. At the funeral. And then when she had come to Jackson Hole in the summer for a visit. Otherwise...it had all been texts and emails and quick phone conversations.

But now that he was back in Texas, he seemed to need to stay for a little while, and she was happy for him to think it was for her. Happy to be the scapegoat so he could work through whatever emotional thing he needed to work through. Knox, in the past, would have been enraged at the assessment that he needed to work through anything emotionally. He was such a stoic guy, always had been.

But she knew he wouldn't even pretend there wasn't lingering damage from the loss of his little girl. Selena had watched him break apart completely at Eleanor's funeral. They had never talked about it again. She didn't think they ever would. But then, she supposed they didn't need to. They had shared the experience. That moment when he couldn't be strong anymore. When there was no child to be strong for, and when his wife had been off with her family, and there had simply been no reason for him to remain standing upright. Selena had been there for that moment.

If all the years of friendship hadn't bonded them, that moment would have done it all on its own.

Just thinking of it made her chest ache, and she shook off the feeling, going over to the coffee maker to pour herself a cup.

She wondered if Knox was still sleeping. He was going to be mad if he missed prime caffeination time.

She wandered out of the kitchen and into the living room just as the door to the guest bedroom opened and Knox walked out, pulling his T-shirt over his head—but not quickly enough. She caught a flash of muscled, tanned skin and…chest hair. Oh, the chest hair. Why was that compelling enough to stop her in her tracks? She didn't even have a moment to question it. She was too caught up. Too beset by the sight.

Genuinely. She was completely immobilized by the sight of her best friend's muscles.

It wasn't like she had never seen Knox shirtless

before. But it had been a long time. And the last time, he had most definitely been married.

Not that she had forgotten he was hot when he was married to Cassandra. It was just that…he had been a married man. And that meant something to Selena. Because it meant something to him.

It had been a barrier, an insurmountable one, even bigger than that whole long-term friendship thing. And now it wasn't there. It just wasn't. He was walking out of the guest bedroom looking sleep rumpled and entirely too lickable. And there was just…nothing stopping them from doing what men and women did.

She'd had a million excuses for *not* doing that. For a long time. She didn't want to risk entanglements, didn't want to compromise her focus. Didn't want to risk pregnancy. Didn't have time for a relationship.

But she was in a place where those things were less of a concern. This house was symbolic of that change in her life. She was making a home. And making a home made her want to fill it. With art, with warmth, with knickknacks that spoke to her. With people.

She wondered, then. What it would be like to actually live with a man? To have one in her life? In her home? In her bed?

And just like that she was fantasizing about Knox in her bed. That body she had caught a glimpse of relaxing beneath her emerald green bedspread, his hands clasped behind his head, a satisfied smile on his face…

She sucked in a sharp breath and tried to get a hold of herself. "Coffee is ready," she said, grinning broadly, not feeling the grin at all.

"Good," he said, his voice rough from sleep.

It struck her then, just what an intimate thing that was. To hear someone's voice after they had been sleeping.

"Right this…way," she said, awkwardly beating a path into the kitchen, turning away from him quickly enough that she sloshed coffee over the edge of her cup.

"You have food for breakfast?" he asked, that voice persistently gravelly and interesting, and much less like her familiar friend's than she would like it to be. She needed some kind of familiarity to latch on to, something to blot out the vision of his muscles. But he wasn't giving her anything.

Jerk.

"No," she said, keeping her voice cheery. "I have coffee and spite for breakfast."

"Well, that's not going to work for me."

"I'm not sure what to tell you," she said, flinging open one of her cabinets and revealing her collection of cereal and biscotti. "Of course I have food for breakfast."

"Bacon? Eggs?"

"Do I look like a diner to you?" she asked.

"Not you personally. But I was hoping that your house might have more diner-like qualities."

"No," she said, opening up the fridge and rummaging around. "Well, what do you know? I *do* have eggs. And bacon. I get a delivery of groceries every week. From a certain grocery store."

He smiled, a lopsided grin that did something to her stomach. Something she was going to ignore and call hunger, because they were talking about bacon, and being hungry for bacon was much more palatable than being hungry for your best friend.

"I'll cook," he said.

"Oh no," she said, getting the package of bacon out of the fridge and handing it to Knox before bending back down and grabbing the carton of eggs and placing that in his other hand. "You don't have to cook."

"Why do I get the feeling that I really do have to cook?"

She shrugged. "It depends on whether you want bacon and eggs."

"Do you not know how to cook?"

"I know how to cook," she said. "But the odds of me actually cooking when I only have half of a cup of coffee in my system are basically none. Usually, I prefer to have sweets for breakfast. Hence, biscotti and breakfast cereals. However, I will sometimes eat bacon and eggs for dinner. Or I will eat bacon and eggs for breakfast if a handsome man fixes them for me."

He lifted a brow. "Oh, I see. So you have this in your fridge for when a man spends the night."

"Obviously. Since a man did just spend the night." Her face flushed. She knew exactly what he was imagining. And really, he had no idea.

That was not why she had the bacon and eggs. She had the bacon and eggs because sometimes she liked an easy dinner. But she didn't really mind if Knox thought she had more of a love life than she actually did.

Of course, now they were thinking about that kind of thing at the same time. Which was…weird. And possibly responsible for the strange electric current arcing between them.

"I'll cook," he said, breaking that arc and moving to the stove, getting out pans and bowls, cracking eggs with an efficiency she admired.

"Do you have an assignment list for me?" he asked, picking up the bowl and whisking the eggs inside.

Why was that sexy? What was happening? His broad shoulders and chest, those intensely muscled forearms, somehow seeming all the more masculine when he was scrambling eggs, of all things.

There was something about the very domestic action, and she couldn't figure out what it was. Maybe it was the contrast between masculinity and domesticity. Or maybe it was just because there had never been a man in her kitchen making breakfast.

She tried to look blasé, as though men made her breakfast every other weekend. After debauchery. Lots and lots of debauchery. She had a feeling she wasn't quite managing blasé, so she just took a sip of her coffee and stared at the white star that hung on her back wall, her homage to the Lone Star State. And currently, her salvation.

"Assignment list," she said, slamming her hands down on the countertop, breaking her reverie. She owed that star a thank-you for restoring her sanity. She'd just needed a moment of not looking at Knox. "Well, I want new hardware on those cabinets. The people who lived here before me had a few things that weren't really to my taste. That is one of them. Also, there are some things in an outbuilding the previous inhabitants left, and I want them moved out. Oh, and I want to get rid of the ceiling fan in the living room."

"I hope you're planning on paying me for this," he said, dumping the eggs into the pan, a sizzling sound filling the room.

"Nope," she said, lifting her coffee mug to her lips.

Knox finished cooking, and somehow Selena managed not to swoon. So, that was good.

They didn't bother to go into her dining room.

Instead they sat at the tall chairs around the island, and Selena looked down at her breakfast resolutely.

"Are you okay?"

"What?" She looked up, her eyes clashing with Knox's. "You keep asking me that."

"Because you keep acting like you might not be."

"Are you okay?"

"I'm alive," he responded. "As to being okay... that's not really part of my five-year plan."

"What's your five-year plan?"

"Not drink myself into a stupor. Keep my business running, because at some point I probably will be glad I still have it. That's about it."

"Well," she said softly, "you can add replacing my kitchen hardware to your five-year plan. But I would prefer it be on this side of it, rather than the back end."

He laughed, and she found that incredibly gratifying. Without thinking, she reached out and brushed her fingertips against his cheek, against his beard. She drew back quickly, wishing the impression of that touch would fade away. It didn't.

"Yes?" he asked.

"Are you keeping the beard?"

"It's not really a fashion statement. It's more evidence of personal neglect."

"Well, you haven't neglected your whole body," she said, thinking of that earlier flash of muscle. She immediately regretted her words. She regretted them more than she did touching his beard. And beard-touching was pretty damned inappropriate between friends. At least, she was pretty certain it was.

He lifted a brow and took a bite of bacon. "Elaborate."

"I'm just saying. You're in good shape, Knox. I noticed."

"Okay," he said slowly, setting the bacon down. His gray eyes were cool as they assessed her, but for some reason she felt heat pooling in her stomach.

Settle down.

Her body did not listen. It kept on being hot. And that heat bled into her cheeks. So she knew she was blushing brilliant rose for Knox's amusement.

"I'm just used to complimenting the men who make me breakfast," she said, doing her best to keep her voice deadpan.

"I see."

"So."

"So," he responded. "There's nothing to do other than work," he said. "Lifting hay bales, fixing fences, basically throwing heavy things around on the ranch. Then going back into the house and working out in the gym. It's all I do."

Well, that explained a few things. "I imagine you could carve out about five minutes to shave."

"Would you prefer that I did?"

"I don't have an opinion on your facial hair."

"You seem to have an opinion on my facial hair."

"I really don't. I had observations about your facial hair, but that's an entirely different thing."

"Somehow, I don't think it is."

"Well, you're entitled to your opinion. About my opinion on your facial hair. Or my lack of one. But that doesn't make it fact."

He shook his head. "You know, if I had you visiting in Jackson Hole I probably wouldn't work out so excessively. Your chatter would keep me busy."

"Hey," she said. "I don't chatter. I'm making conversation." Except, it sounded a whole lot like chatter, even to herself.

"Okay."

She made a coughing sound and stood up, taking her mostly empty plate to the sink and then making her way back toward the living room, stepping over her discarded high heels from yesterday. She heard the sound of Knox's bare feet on the floor behind her. And suddenly, the fact that he had bare feet seemed intimate.

You really have been a virgin for too long.

She grimaced, even as she chastised herself. She hated that word. She hated even thinking it. It implied a kind of innocence she didn't possess. Also, it felt young. She was not particularly young. She had just been busy. Busy, and resolutely opposed to relationships.

Still, the whole virginity thing had the terrible

side effect of making rusty morning voices and bare feet seem intimate.

She looked up and out the window and saw her car in the driveway. "Hey," she said. "How did that happen?"

"I told you I was going to take care of it. Ye of little faith."

"Apparently, Knox, you can't even take care of your beard, so why would I think you would take care of my car so efficiently?"

"Correction," he said. "I don't bother to make time to shave my beard. Why? Because I don't *have* to. Because I'm not beholden to anyone anymore."

Those words were hollow, even though he spoke them in a light tone. And no matter how he would try and spin it, he didn't feel it was a positive thing. It seemed desperately sad that nobody in his life cared whether or not he had a beard.

"I like it," she said finally.

She did. He was hot without one, too. He had one of those square Hollywood jaws and a perfectly proportioned chin. And if asked prior to seeing him with the beard, she would have said facial hair would have been like hiding his light under a bushel.

But in reality, the beard just made him look… more masculine. Untamed. Rugged. Sexy.

Yes. Sexy.

She cleared her throat. "Anyway," she said. "I won't talk about it anymore."

Suddenly, she realized Knox was standing much closer to her than she'd been aware of until a moment ago. She could smell some kind of masculine body wash and clean, male skin. And she could feel the heat radiating from his body. If she reached out, she wouldn't even have to stretch her arm out to press her palm against his chest. Or to touch his beard again, which she had already established was completely inappropriate, but she was thinking about it anyway.

"You like it?" he asked, his voice getting rougher, even more than it had been this morning when he had first woken up.

"I… Yes?"

"You're not sure?"

"No," she said, taking a step toward him, her feet acting entirely on their own and without permission from her brain. "No, I'm sure. I like it."

She felt weightless, breathless. She felt a little bit like leaning toward him and seeing what might happen if she closed that space between them. Seeing how that beard might feel if it was pressed against her cheek, what it might feel like if his mouth was pressed against hers…

She was insane. She was officially insane. She was checking out her friend. Her grieving friend who needed her to be supportive and not lecherous.

She shook her head and took a step back. "Thank you," she said. Instead of kissing him. Instead of doing anything crazy. "For making sure the car got back to me. Really, thank you for catching me when I passed out yesterday. I think I'm still…you know."

"No," he said, crossing his muscular arms over his broad chest. "I'm not sure that I do know."

Freaking Knox. Not helping her out at all. "I think I'm still a little bit spacey," she said.

"Understandable. Hey, direct me to your hardware, and I'll get started on that."

Okay, maybe he was going to help her out. She was going to take that lifeline with both hands. "I can do that," she said, and she rushed to oblige him.

Four

Knox was almost completely finished replacing the hardware in Selena's kitchen when the phone in his pocket vibrated. He frowned, the number coming up one he didn't recognize.

He answered it and lifted it to his ear. "Knox McCoy," he said.

"Hi there, Knox" came the sound of an older woman's voice on the other end of the line. She had a thick East Texas drawl and a steel thread winding through the greeting that indicated she wasn't one to waste a word or spare a feeling. "I'm Cora Lee. Will's stepmother. I'm not sure if he's ever mentioned me."

"Will and I haven't been close for the past decade or so," he said honestly. Really, the falling-out between Will and Selena had profoundly affected his friendship with the other man.

In divorces, friends chose sides. And his side had always clearly been Selena's.

"Still," Cora Lee said, "there's nothing like coming back from the dead to patch up old relationships. And, on that subject, I would like to have a small get-together to celebrate Will's return, just for those of us who were at the service. You can imagine that we're all thrilled."

If she was thrilled, Knox wouldn't have been able to tell by her tone of voice. She was more resolute. Determined. And he had a feeling that refusing her would be a lot like saying no to a drill sergeant.

"It will be kind of like a funeral, only celebrating that he's not dead. And you'll be invited. He said he wanted you to come."

"He did?"

"Not in so many words, but I feel like it is what he wants." And Knox had a feeling it wouldn't matter if Will did want it or not. Cora Lee was going to do exactly what she thought was best. "And he wants that ex-wife of his to come, too. He says you two are close."

"Which ex-wife?" He had gotten the distinct impression that there was more than one former Mrs. Sanders floating around.

"The one you're close to," Cora Lee responded, her voice deadpan.

Reluctantly, Knox decided he liked Will's step-mother. "Well, I'll let her know. She went to the funeral, so I imagine she'll want to go to this." He wasn't sure he particularly wanted to, but if Selena was going, then he would accompany her. He was honestly concerned that the other women who had been named beneficiaries, or whoever was respon-sible for sending the letter, might take advantage of a situation like this.

"Good. I'll put you both down on the guest list, and I'll send details along shortly. You have to come, because I wrote your names down and there will be too much brisket if you don't."

And with that, she hung up the phone. He looked down at the screen for a moment, and then Selena came in, her footsteps soft on the hardwood floor.

He looked up and his stomach tightened. Her long black hair was wet, as though she'd gotten out of the shower, and he suddenly became very aware of the fact that her gray T-shirt was clinging to her curves a little bit more than it might if her skin wasn't damp. Which put him in mind to think about the fact that her skin was damp, which meant it had been uncov-ered only a few moments before.

What the hell was wrong with him? He was think-ing like a horny teenager. Yeah, it had been a few years since he'd had sex, but frankly, he hadn't wanted to. His libido had been hibernating, along with his desire to do basic things like shave his beard.

But somehow it seemed to be stirring to life again, and it was happening at a very inappropriate time, with an inappropriate person.

The good thing was that it must be happening around Selena because she was the only woman in proximity, and it was about time he started to feel again. The bad thing was...Selena was the only woman in proximity.

"Who was that on the phone?" she asked, running her fingers through her hair.

"Will's stepmother. She wants us to go to a non-funeral for him in a few days."

"Oh."

She was frowning, a small crinkle appearing on her otherwise smooth forehead.

"Something wrong?"

"No. It's a good thing. I'm glad to be asked. I mean, I was thinking, when I assumed he was dead, that it was so sad he and I had never...that we had never found a way to fix our friendship."

"You want to do that?" He was surprised.

"It seems silly to stay mad at somebody over something that happened so long ago. Something I know neither of us would change."

"The marriage?"

She laughed. "The divorce. I don't regret the divorce, so there's really no point in being upset about it. Or avoiding him forever because of it. I mean, obviously there was conflict surrounding it." She looked away, a strange, tight expression on her face. "But if neither of us would go back and change the outcome, I don't see why we can't let it go. I would like to let it go. It was terrible, thinking he was dead and knowing we had never reconciled."

Knox pressed his hand to his chest and rubbed the spot over his heart. It twinged a little. But that was nothing new. It did that sometimes. At first, he had thought he was having a heart attack. But then, in the beginning, it had been much worse. Suffocating, deep, sharp pain.

Something that took his breath away.

No one had ever told him that grief hurt. That it was a physical pain. That the depression that lingered on after would hurt all the way down to your bones. That sometimes you would wake up in the middle of the night and not be able to breathe.

Those were the kinds of things people didn't tell you. But then, there was no guidebook for loss like he had experienced. Actually, there was. There were tons of books about it. But there had been no reason in hell for him to go out and buy one. Not before it had happened, and then when Eleanor had gotten sick, he hadn't wanted to do doomsday preparation for the loss he still didn't want to believe was inevitable.

Afterward...

He was in the shit whether he wanted to be or not. So he didn't see the point of trying to figure out a way to navigate more elegantly through it. Shit was shit. There was no dressing it up.

There was just doing your best to put one foot in front of the other and walk on through.

But he had walked through it alone, and in the end that had been too much for him and Cassandra. But he hadn't known how to do it with another person. Hadn't really wanted to.

Hadn't known how he was supposed to look at the mother of his dead child and offer her comfort, tell her that everything was going to be okay, that *anything* was going to be okay.

But now they had disentangled themselves from each other, and still this thing Selena was talking about, this desire for reconciliation, just didn't resonate with him. He didn't want to talk to Cassandra. It was why they were divorced.

"It's not the same thing," she said, her voice suddenly taking on that soft, careful quality that appeared in people's tones when they were dancing around the subject of his loss. "Mine and Will's relationship. It's not the same as yours and Cassandra's. It's not the same as your divorce. Will and I were married for a year. We were young, we were selfish and we were stupid. The two of you… You built a life together. And then you lost it. You went through hell. It's just not the same thing. So don't think I'm lecturing you subtly on how you should call her or something."

"I didn't think that."

"You did a little. Or you were making yourself feel guilty about it, and that isn't fair. You don't deserve that."

She was looking at him with a sweet, freshly scrubbed openness that made his stomach go tight. Made him want to lift up his coffee mug and throw it down onto the tile, just to make the feeling stop. Made him want to grab hold of her face, hold her steady and kiss her mouth. So she would shut up. So she would stop being so understanding. So she would stop looking at him and seeing him. Seeing inside of him.

That thought, hot and destructive, made his veins feel full of fire rather than blood. And he wasn't sure anymore what his motivation actually was. To get her to stop, or to just exorcise the strange demon that seemed to have possessed him at some point between the moment he had held her in his arms on the floor of the funeral home and when they had come back here.

He had his life torn apart once, and he wasn't in a hurry to tear up the good that was left. At least, that was what he would have said, but this destructive urge had overtaken him. And his primary thought was to either break something or grab hold of her.

He needed to do more manual labor. Obviously.

"I'm not sure you're in a great position to speak about what I do and don't deserve," he said, the words coming out harder than he'd intended.

"Except you're here at my house because you want to protect me, and you just replaced all my cabinet hardware, and it looks amazing. So I guess I would say you deserve pretty good things, since you're obviously a pretty good guy."

"Cabinet hardware isn't exactly a ringing endorsement on character," he said.

He needed to get some distance between them, because he was being a dick. It was uncalled-for. Selena wasn't responsible for his baggage. Not for making him feel better about it, not for carrying any of the weight.

"What about the work you need done outside?" he asked.

"Sorting through the shed. But we're going to need a truck for that."

"Do you have one?"

"I actually do. But I don't drive it very much."

"Why do you have a truck?"

"Extravagance?"

He didn't believe her, since Selena didn't do much for the sake of extravagance. If she had wanted to do something extravagant, he knew she could've gotten herself a big McMansion in town. Some eyesore at the end of a cul-de-sac. God knew she made enough money with that skin-care line of hers. But instead she had buried herself out here in the boonies, gotten herself this little cabin that wouldn't be extravagant by anyone's standard.

"To try and make friends," she said. "It's really helpful when you have something for people to use when they move. You'd be surprised how popular it makes you."

"Honey, this is Texas. I don't think there are enough people around without a pickup for that to be true."

"You'd be surprised," she said. "And my best friend hasn't been back to Texas in so long that I had to resort to making new friends any way I could."

Now she was making him feel guilty. As if he didn't already feel guilty about the illicit thoughts he'd just had about her.

"Well, you're probably better off," he said, keeping his tone light, brushing past her and heading out the front door.

To his chagrin, she followed him, scampering like a woodland creature out onto the porch behind him. "I don't know about that."

"Do you have the keys to the truck?"

"I can grab them," she said.

For some reason, he had a feeling she was stalling, and he couldn't figure out why. "Can I have them?"

"How about I go with you?"

"Don't you have other things to do? As you reminded me yesterday, you have your own money, and therefore don't need Will's estate, because you're a multimillionaire. Not from nothing, though. You actually run a giant business."

"We both do. And yet here we are. I can afford to take some time off to visit with you, Knox."

That made him feel like an ass. Because he was trying to put some distance between them.

All you do is put distance between yourself and people these days.

Well, he could do without that cutting observation from his own damn self.

"Fine." He didn't mean to grunt the word, but he did, and Selena pretended to ignore it as she went back in the house, reappearing a minute later with keys dangling from her fingertips.

She was grinning, to compensate for his scowl, he had a feeling.

"I will direct you to the truck," she said, keeping that grin sparkly and very much in place.

"You made it sound like you had an old pickup truck lying around," he said when they approached the shiny red and very new vehicle parked out back.

"I told you I bought it partly for extravagance. I couldn't resist."

Unlike himself, Selena had actually grown up with money, but he had always gotten the feeling her father had kept a tight leash on her. So whatever cash had been at her disposal hadn't really been hers; her life hadn't really been hers.

In contrast, he had grown up with nothing.

No support. No parent who had even bothered to try and be controlling, because they hadn't cared enough.

All in all, it was tough to say which of them had had it worse.

"Just because?"

"Because I do what I want," she said, confirming his earlier thought.

"Yes, you certainly do," he said.

She always had. From going to school, starting her own business, marrying Will when it had seemed like such a crazy thing to do. They had still been at Harvard at the time, and he hadn't seen the damned point in rushing anything.

But she had been determined. And when Selena Jacobs was determined, there was no stopping her.

"I'll drive," she said.

He reached out and snatched the keys from her hand. "I'll drive."

"It's my truck," she protested.

He paused, leaning down toward her, ignoring the tightening feeling in his stomach. And lower. "And I'm the man, baby."

She laughed in his face. He deserved it, he had to admit. But he was still fucking driving.

"That does not mean you get to drive."

"In this case it does," he said, jerking open the passenger-side door and holding it for her.

She gave him the evil eye, but got into the truck, sitting primly and waiting for him to close the door.

He rounded to the driver's side and got in, looking down at the cup holders, both of which contained two partly finished smoothies of indeterminate age. "Really?" he asked, looking down at the cups.

"I have a housekeeper," she said. "Not a truck keeper."

He grunted. "Now, where am I going?"

"You should have let me drive," she said, leaning toward him. And suddenly, it felt like high school. Being in the cab of the truck with a girl who made it difficult to breathe, knowing what he wanted to do next and knowing that he probably couldn't.

Except back then, he would have done the ill-advised thing. The dick-motivated thing. Because back then he didn't think too far ahead.

Well, except for two things. Getting the grades he needed for a scholarship to Harvard and getting laid.

Those things were a lot more compatible than people might realize. And the bad-boy facade made it easy to hide the fact that he was on a specific academic track. Which had been good, in his estimation. Because if he had failed and ended up pumping gas, no one would have been the wiser. No one would have known that he'd had a different dream. That he'd wanted anything at all beyond the small Texas town he had grown up in.

Fortunately, Harvard had worked out.

He had become a success, as far as everyone was concerned.

He wondered how they talked about him in Royal now. Probably a cautionary tale. Evidence of the fact that at the end of the day not even money could protect you from the harsh realities of life.

That you bled and hurt and died like everyone else.

All in all, it wasn't exactly the legend he had hoped to create for himself.

After Eleanor's funeral, someone had told him that you couldn't have everything. He had punched that person in the face.

"Just head that way," she said, waving her hand, clearly not too bothered with being specific in her directions.

He drove across the flat, bumpy property until he saw a shed in the distance, a small building that clearly predated the house by the river. He wondered if it had been the original home.

"Is this it?" he asked.

"If I were driving, you wouldn't have to ask."

"You are a prickly little cuss," he said, pulling up to the outbuilding and putting the truck in Park.

"It's good for the pores," she said, sniffing.

"So it's not all your magic Clarity skin care?"

"That works, too, but you know, a healthy lifestyle complements all skin-care regimens," she said, sounding arch. Then she smiled broadly, all white teeth and golden skin, looking every inch the savvy spokeswoman that she was.

"Question," he said as they got out of the truck.

"Possible answer," she quipped as the two of them walked to the shed.

"Why skin-care products? Is that your passion?"

"Why organic food?" she shot back.

"That's an easy answer," he returned. "That mom-and-pop place I used to go to for deli food when I had a late-night study session was doing crazy business. And it didn't make any sense to me why. When they wanted to retire, I ended up talking to the owner about the business. And how good food, health food, was an expanding market. I mean, I didn't care that it was healthy—I was in my early twenties. I just liked the macaroni and cheese. I didn't care that it was from a locally sourced dairy. So when the opportunity came to buy the shop, I took it. It was a risky business, and I knew it. It could have gone either way. But it ended up growing. And growing. And before I knew it, I owned a chain of grocery stores. And it became a billion-dollar industry. All because I liked the macaroni and cheese."

They got out of the truck, slamming the doors in tandem. He looked around at the scenery. He could see why Selena had bought the place. It was quiet.

Remote, like his ranch in Wyoming. There was something to be said for that. For being able to go off grid. For being able to get some quiet.

"Now you," he said, prompting her.

She wrinkled her nose, twisting her lips to one side. "I guess it's similar for me. I knew I wanted a business that was mine. I knew I wanted to do something that was under my control. And I did a lot of research about profit margins and low overhead start-up. You know I got a business degree, and I also took all of that chemistry. Just as a minor. The two things are compatible. Skin care and chemistry. And like you said, natural organic products were on the upswing."

"So you're not particularly passionate about skin care."

She lifted a shoulder. "I find that you can easily become passionate about a great many different things. I love having my own money. I love controlling my life. I really like the fact that what I do empowers women in some regard. Skin care is not a necessity, but it's nice. When you feel good about yourself, I think you can do more with your life. Mostly, my passion is in the success." She smiled. "I feel like you can relate to that."

He wasn't sure. Things had changed for him so dramatically over the past few years. "Once you make a certain amount of money, though," he said, flinging the doors to the shed open, "it really is just more money."

"More security," she said. "All of this has to go." She waved a hand around as if it was a magic wand that might make the items disappear.

He looked down at her and smiled. She was such an imperious little thing. Sometimes he could definitely tell she had come from a wealthy family, a privileged background. She gave an order, and she expected to be followed. Or maybe that was just Selena.

"Not necessarily," he said, the words coming out a lot more heavily than he'd intended as he picked up what he thought might be part of an old rocking chair.

"I'm sorry" came Selena's muted reply. "I wasn't thinking when I said that."

"I wasn't thinking of the past either," he said. "It's just that money doesn't let you control the whole world, Selena. That's a fact."

"Well, my father sure thinks it does. And he thought he could use it to control me." She cleared her throat. "That was why… It was why I had to marry Will."

Those words hit him square in the chest, almost like one of the large stacks had fallen square on him. "What do you mean you had to marry him?"

"I just… My grandfather died my freshman year. Do you remember that?"

"Of course I remember that. You were distraught."

She sucked in a deep breath. "He was the only

person who ever believed in me, Knox. He was the only person who acted like I could do something. Be something. I loved him. So much. He was also definitely an antique. And there was a trust fund. A trust fund that was set aside for me, but I couldn't access it until I was twenty-five, which was when he figured I would be an adult. Really."

"Twenty-five? That seems…"

"Or I could have gotten married." She looked up at him then, her eyes full of meaning. "Which is what I did."

Her meaning hit him with the force of a slap. He was in shock. And the way he responded to that feeling was by getting mad. He growled and walked out of the shed, heading toward the pickup and flinging the piece of chair into the truck bed. Then he stalked back inside and picked up something else, didn't matter particularly to him what it was. "So you had to marry him because you needed the money?" he asked finally, his heart pounding so hard he was sure it would gallop out of his chest.

All this time he'd thought she'd fallen in love with Will. And that had truly put her off-limits, even after the marriage ended. She had chosen another man when Knox was right there. There wasn't a stronger way to telegraph disinterest.

Their friendship had been too important, way too important, to act on any attraction on his end.

Particularly when she'd made it clear how she felt when she'd married Will.

Except she hadn't loved Will. Hadn't wanted him.

"Yes," she said. "I remember that you thought it was crazy when we got married. When we didn't just live together. Well, that was why."

"You didn't tell me," he said, his tone fierce and a hell of a lot angrier than he'd intended it to be. "I'm supposed to be your best friend, Selena, and you didn't tell me what was happening?"

"You had your own stuff, Knox. You were dealing with school. And you were on a scholarship to be there. I didn't want to do anything that would interfere with your grades. And that included bringing you into my drama."

"I was your best friend," he reiterated. "I've always taken your drama. That's how it works. How the hell could you underestimate me like that?" He shook his head. "No wonder the two of you got divorced. You married because of a trust fund."

"I don't want to rehash the past with you," she snarled, picking up a bicycle tire and stomping out of the shed. "It doesn't matter. It doesn't matter what happened between me and Will. Not now. The marriage ended, end of story. It was definitely a bad idea. Don't you think I know that? We divorced. It completely ruined our friendship."

"Why?"

"Are you and Cassandra friends?" she asked.

"No," he said. "But as you have pointed out several times, my marriage to Cassandra was not the same as your marriage to Will. So let's not pretend now. Why did it ruin your friendship with Will?"

She bristled visibly. "Because of Rich Lowell."

"That guy who used to follow Will around? The tool with the massive crush on you?"

"That tool only got interested in me when he thought Will was. And after we married he said some things to me... They didn't seem completely far-fetched. He asked me why Will would suddenly want me when... when he didn't before. He implied Will only wanted my money. Of course, Rich didn't know the details of the trust fund, he only knew I came from a wealthy family, but he made me question... Why would Will agree to marry me only to help me get my trust fund? It was so hard for me to believe he was doing it because he was my friend. That he was doing it because he cared about me. I couldn't imagine anyone doing that.

"When you grow up the way I did... When you have to walk on eggshells around your father, you kind of fold in on yourself. And you focus on surviving. That was what I did. I became this creature who only knew how to scrabble forward. I was selfish, and I couldn't imagine anyone *not* being selfish. So when Rich asked me those questions...it just seemed more likely that Will wanted something from me than that he actually wanted to help me. I got mad at Will. I told him I didn't want anything to do with him. That if he thought he was getting any of my money he was completely insane." She laughed, the sound watery. "You know, that's why it was extra hilarious that he left me that inheritance. I mean, I guess he didn't. Because he wasn't dead. Because he didn't even really write the letter."

Knox had some sympathy for her. He truly did. Because he could remember Selena as she had been. It had been so hard for her to trust. So difficult for her to believe anyone wanted anything for her that wasn't a benefit to themselves.

For a kid from the wrong side of the tracks, knowing Selena had been somewhat eye-opening. He'd discovered that people who lived on the other side of the poverty line still had problems. They could be half-feral. They could be insecure. They could have real, serious life-and-death problems. He had always imagined that if he had money he could buy off all of life's bullshit. Meeting Selena had been his first realization that wasn't the case.

But even with the sympathy he felt, there was anger. So much damned anger. Because he hadn't deserved to be lied to for the better part of the last decade. She had never told him any of the truth, and he couldn't quite stomach that.

The nature of her relationship with Will had always been a secret from him.

He whirled around to face her and she squeaked,

taking three steps backward, her shoulder blades butting against the side of the shed.

"You lied to me," he said.

"Well," she shot back, her acerbic tone reminding him of the past. "I didn't realize all of my baggage affected your daily life to this degree, Knox."

"You know it doesn't," he said.

"So why are you acting like it does? Why are you acting like it matters at all? It doesn't. It's ancient history. If I'm not upset about it anymore, then why are you?"

"Obviously, you and Will are upset about it, or the two of you would still speak to each other."

"The rift in our friendship has nothing to do with our divorce. It has everything to do with the fact that I accused him of being a gold digger." She sighed heavily. "You can imagine he was not thrilled with that. He pointed out that he didn't need money, of course. And I said being from rich parents didn't mean you didn't need money. I was exhibit A."

"I understand why that would bother him, but he couldn't forgive you for that? Will was not the kind of guy who took himself that seriously back then, and I can't imagine he's changed all that much in the years since."

She grimaced. "I never asked him to."

"You never asked him to forgive you?" he asked, incredulous. "Even though you accused him of something when he was trying to help you?"

She made a sound that was halfway between a growl and a squeak. "It doesn't matter."

"Then why are you so defensive about it?"

"Why are you acting like this? You're pissed because I didn't talk to you?"

"Because you didn't trust me," he said, moving nearer to her.

She shrank back slightly, turning her head. And her reaction just about sent him over the edge. He knew she'd had a rough past, but that was a long time ago. And he was not her father. He didn't use physical threats to intimidate women, and he had damn sure never done it to her.

He had been nothing but careful with her. And she had lied to him all these years about her feelings for Will. She hadn't trusted Knox back then. And she was acting like he might do something to hurt her now, when he was here because he wanted to make sure that she was safe and protected.

He reached out, gripping her chin with his thumb and forefinger, forcing her to look up at him. "Don't act like that," he said, his voice hard. "Don't look at me like I'm a damn stranger."

She tilted her chin up, her expression defiant. And then the wind picked up and he caught that sweet smell that spoke *Selena* to him. Lavender and the Texas breeze, and why the hell that should affect him, he didn't know. But it did.

"Then don't act like a stranger," she said.

His blood reached the boiling point then, and before he knew what he was doing, he had leaned in closer, his nose scant inches from hers. "I'm not acting like one," he said, his voice rough. "But I'm about to."

She had never really wanted Will. She had never chosen Will over Knox.

That changed things.

And then he closed the distance between them and pressed his lips to hers.

Five

Knox was kissing her.

She was sure she was dreaming. Except it was nothing like one of her typical dreams. In those fantasies—which she had always been quite ashamed of—they were always having some nice moment, and then he would capture her lips gently with his before pulling her into his warm, comforting embrace.

In those fantasies, he always looked at her with his lovely gray eyes, and they would soften with warmth and affection before he would lean in.

In this reality, his gray eyes had been hard. He had not been smiling at her. And his lips were… This was not a sweet foray over the line of friendship. No.

This was some kind of barbarous conquering of her mouth by his.

This was an invasion. And there were no questions being asked. He was still holding her chin, the impression of his thumb digging into her skin as he tugged down and opened her mouth wide, angling his head and dipping his tongue deep. Sliding it against hers. And she wanted to pull away. She wanted to be angry. Wanted to be indignant.

Because he was angry at her, and he'd been yelling at her. And she was angry at him. He had no right to question her when he had no real idea of what she had lived through. No real idea of what she'd been trying to escape.

Not when he had no idea that the reason she hadn't told him the truth wasn't because she didn't trust him, but because she didn't trust herself. Because what she had really wanted to do, even back then, was ask *Knox* to marry her. But she had known, deep down inside, that with him, a marriage could never be fake. That with him, she would always want everything. And his friendship was so special, she had never wanted to risk it.

Her feelings for him had always been big. Somehow, she had known instinctively that if she made him her husband it would be easy for him to become everything. As painful as it had been, as suspicious and horrible as she'd behaved with Will over their friendship...

Giving in to wanting Knox, to having him…that would have destroyed the girl she'd been.

So she'd kept a distance between them. She'd done what she'd had to do to guard her heart and their friendship. And now he was demolishing all of that good work. That restraint she had shown, that diligence she had practiced all these years.

She was furious. Something more than furious. Something deeper. Something that compelled her to do what she decided to do next.

She shifted, grabbing fistfuls of his shirt, and angled her head, tasting him.

Because it wasn't fair that he was the one who had done this. When she was the one who had spent so long behaving. When she was the one who had worked so hard to protect what they had—to protect herself.

He had no regard for her. No regard for her work.

And he had to be punished for that.

She nipped his lower lip and he growled, pressing his hard chest against her breasts as he pinned her to the side of the shed. He gathered her hands, easily wrapping one of his hands around both her wrists, holding them together and drawing her arms up over her head against the wall.

Bastard.

He was trying to take control of this. Trying to take control of her.

No. He was the one who was ruining things. He

was the one ruining *them*. She hadn't gotten the chance to do it. She had been good. She had done her best. And now he wanted all the control?

No. Absolutely not.

She bit him again. This time her teeth scraped hard across his lower lip, and he growled louder, pressing her harder against the wall.

His teeth ran across the bottom of her lip. He nipped her. And somehow, the anger drained out of her.

There was something primal about having her best friend's tongue in her mouth. She had to simply surrender. That was all. Beginning and end.

A wave of emotion washed over her, a wave of need. The entire ocean she had been holding back for more than a decade.

Knox. It had always been Knox that she wanted. Always.

She had messed up everything when she married Will. *Everything.* And when they had divorced it had been too late. Knox had been with Cassandra. And their relationship had been real and serious.

That still bothered her. He had found something real with someone else. She never had.

It would never be the same. Because she had never... She had never loved anyone but him.

And he had loved someone else.

That internal admission hurt. More than that, it

made her heart feel like it could shatter into a million pieces with each beat.

But then it just beat harder, faster as Knox shifted, curving his arm around her waist and drawing her against him. She could feel his hardness. Could feel the insistent press of him against her hip that told her this kiss wasn't about teaching her a lesson. Wasn't about anger.

Yes, it had started with anger. But now it was just need. Deep, carnal need between two people who knew each other. Two people who knew exactly what each had been through. There were no explanations required between her and Knox.

That isn't true. There are no explanations required on his end. But I haven't been honest with him. And he knows it. It's why he's angry.

She squeezed her eyes shut and ignored that internal admonishment, parting her lips and kissing Knox deeper, harder.

She was ready for this. Ready to let him undo her jeans, push them down her thighs and take her virginity right there against the side of the shed.

And there was a phrase she had never imagined herself thinking.

Her virginity. Oh, *damn it*. That would be a whole other conversation.

But then suddenly, the conversation became irrelevant, because Knox wrenched his mouth away from hers and wheeled back, his lips set in a grim line, those gray eyes harder than she could ever remember seeing them.

"What?" she asked, breathing heavily, trying to act as though her world hadn't just been tilted on its axis.

"What the hell?"

"You kissed me, Knox. You got mad at me and you kissed me. I'm sure there's some kind of Freudian horror that explains that kind of behavior, but I don't know it."

"You bit me," he pointed out.

"And you pinned my wrists against the wall." She gritted her teeth and turned away from him, hoping to hide the mounting color in her cheeks. Hoping he wouldn't know just how affected she had been by the whole thing. She was dying. Her heart was about to claw its way out of her mouth, her stomach was turning itself over, and she was so wet between her thighs she didn't think she would ever live down the embarrassment if he found out.

"I didn't realize," he said.

"That you pinned my hands?"

"That *that* was there."

"What? Attraction?" She tried to laugh. "You're a hot guy, Knox. And I'm not immune to that. I mean, maybe I'm not up to your usual standards…"

"What usual standards?" he asked. "I was married for ten years, Selena. I had one standard. The person I made vows to. I haven't been with anyone since."

"Oh," she said. "So I guess that explains it." Her stomach twisted in disappointment, then did a free fall down to her toes. "You are super hard up."

"I was angry," he said.

"Awesome," she said, planting her hands on her hips. "Angry and hard up apparently translates into kissing women you didn't know you were attracted to!"

"I knew I was attracted to you," he said. "But I don't dwell on it."

She paused for a moment, tilting her head to the side. "You…knew you were attracted to me."

"Yes. I have been. Since college. But there's never been any point in exploring that attraction, Selena. You were not in a space to take that on when we first met."

She knew what he was saying was true. She had been attracted to him from the moment they'd met, too, but she'd also built a big wall around herself for a reason.

"I wanted to focus on school," she said, the words sounding lame.

"Until Will and a trust fund came into play?"

"Whatever. You didn't make a move on me. And then our friendship became the thing. And…our friendship is still the thing." No point spilling her guts about what a sad, insecure person she was.

"Yes," he said.

"That's good. I can have sex with any guy," she said, waving her hand as if she had simply hundreds of men to choose from to satisfy her appetites. "You're my only best friend. You've known me for so long and let's just not... Let's not make it weird."

"I just think..."

"You haven't had sex in a while—I get it," she said. Which was pretty damned laughable since she hadn't had sex ever and he was the one who had jumped on her.

"I'd like to think there was more to it than that," he said. "Because there's more to us than that."

She lifted a shoulder. "Fine. Whatever. I'm not that bothered by it. It was just a kiss. Nothing I can't handle."

She was dying inside. Her head was spinning and she was sure she was close to passing out. She would be damned if she would betray all those feelings to him.

She felt like her top layer had been scraped back, like she was dangerously close to being exposed. All of her secrets. All of herself.

She cared about Knox, she really did, but she kept certain things to herself. And he was poking at them.

"So that's it?" he asked. "We kiss after all these years of friendship and you're fine."

"Would you rather I light myself on fire and jump into the river screaming?"

"No," he said closely, "and that's an awfully specific response."

"Knox," she said, "you don't want me to be anything but fine. Believe me. It's better for the two of us if we just move on like nothing happened. I don't think either of us needs this right now."

Or ever.

She wanted to hide. But she knew that if she did hide, it would only let him know how closely he'd delved into things she didn't want him anywhere near. Things she didn't want anyone near.

"Yeah," he said. "I guess so."

"You don't want to talk about our feelings, do you?" she asked, knowing she sounded testy.

"Absolutely not. I've had enough feelings for a lifetime."

"I'm right there with you. I don't have any interest in messing up a good friendship over a little bit of sex."

Knox walked past her, moving back into the shed. Then he paused, kicking his head back out of the doorway. "I agree with you, Selena, except for one little thing. With me, there wouldn't be anything little about the sex."

Knox wasn't sure what had driven him to make that parting comment to Selena after they had kissed against the shed wall. But she had been acting strange and skittish around him ever since.

Not that he could blame her. He had no idea what in hell he'd been thinking.

Except that even though he was angry at her, she also looked soft, and tempting, and delicious. Finding out she had violated his trust, that there were things about her he didn't know, made him feel like their friendship was not quite what he had imagined it was. And in light of that realization, it had been difficult for him to figure out why he shouldn't just kiss her.

Asshole reasoning, maybe, but it had all made perfect sense in the moment. In the moment when he had brought his lips down on hers.

Yeah, it had all made perfect sense then.

The next few days had been incredibly tense, in a way that things never usually were between them. But he could at least appreciate the tension as a distraction from his real life. It was strange, staying with Selena like this in close quarters—that kiss notwithstanding. Because it reminded him a lot of their Harvard days. It wasn't like he'd been blind to how gorgeous she was then. But he'd made a decision about how to treat their friendship, due in large part to Will.

In many ways that decision had made things simple. Though the kiss was complicated, it was nothing compared to loss or divorce or any of the other things he had been through since.

But now they had that party for Will, and they

had to actually go be in public together. And she had to try and act like she was at ease with him rather than looking at him like he might bite her again.

Though *she* had started the biting.

Knox buttoned up his dark blue shirt and tried not to think overly hard about all the biting. And the fact that it had surprised him in a not-unpleasant way.

Damn. He really *did* need to find a woman.

But every time he thought about doing that he just felt tired. He didn't want to cruise bars. He didn't want to find strangers to hook up with.

If he was that desperate for an orgasm he could use his right hand.

He had been in love with Cassandra, once upon a time. Though it was hard to remember the good times. Not because they had faded into memory, but because they hurt.

They also ruined the idea of anonymous sex for him.

He was over that. Done with it. He knew what sex could be like when you *knew* someone. When you had a connection with them. He didn't have any interest in going back to the alternative.

He knew a lot of guys who would kill to be in his position. Away from the commitments of marriage. Knox just didn't see the appeal.

He had never found it monotonous to be with the same person. He had thought it offered far more than it took. To know somebody well enough that you could be confident they were asking for what they wanted. To just know what they wanted at a certain point.

He'd been with his wife for over a decade. The only woman for all that time. It had never seemed a chore to him.

The idea of hooking up—that seemed like a chore.

But damn, he needed to get laid. He was fantasizing about getting bitten by his best friend, so obviously something had to change.

That was the funny thing. Because while he remembered and appreciated the married sex he'd had with Cassandra, he didn't specifically fantasize about *her*. Possibly because she was bound up in something too painful for him to fully relive.

He and Cassandra were over. Done. Everything in him was done with what they'd had.

But he still found himself in the midst of a sex paradox.

He gritted his teeth, walked out of the bedroom he was occupying at Selena's and stopped still.

She was standing in the middle of the living room wearing a bright red dress that conformed to her glorious figure. Her long black hair was styled in loose waves around her shoulders, and she had a flower pinned on the side, part of her hair swept back off her face. She looked beautiful, and effortless, which he knew wasn't the case.

She had spent a good while affecting that look, but she did a damned good impression of someone who hadn't tried at all.

He wanted to kiss the crimson lip color right off her mouth. Wanted to pull her into his arms and re-live the other day.

And he knew he couldn't. Knew he couldn't touch her again, and he couldn't look like he was standing there thinking about it, because they had to get to that party. And he had to manage to get there in one piece, without Selena chewing him up and spitting him out because he was acting like an ass.

He reached over and grabbed his black cowboy hat off the shelf by the door. "I'm ready," he said, positioning it on his head. "Are you?"

"You're wearing jeans," she said.

He lifted a brow. "I'm a cowboy, honey. We wear jeans to parties. Plus, it's Texas."

"I'm wearing *heels*," she said, sticking out one dainty foot and showing off the red stilettos and matching toenail polish on her feet. As if he hadn't already taken stock of that already, with great inter-est. "The least you could have done was throw on a pair of dress pants."

"I have cowboy boots on," he returned. Then he stuck his arm out, offering it to her. "You go with me as is or you go by yourself, babe. Up to you."

She sighed, an exasperated sound, and reached out, taking hold of his arm before moving to the front door with him. This was the first time she had touched him since the kiss. And damn it all if he didn't feel a hard shock of pleasure at the delicate contact of her hand against his arm, even though it was through fabric.

Selena, for her part, seemed unaffected. Or at least, she was doing a good impersonation of someone who was.

"I'll drive," she said, producing her keys and moving to her little red car before he could protest. He had a feeling he would hate butting up against Selena's temper right about now even more than he hated letting someone else drive, so he didn't fight her on it.

"You can drive in those shoes?" he asked when Selena turned the car out onto the highway.

She waved a hand. "You know, Ginger Rogers did everything Fred Astaire did backward and in heels. I can drive a car in stilettos, Knox," she said, her tone crisp and dry like a good Chardonnay.

He would like very much to take a sip of her.

"Good to know," he said.

"You're not impressed with my logic," she said, sounding petulant.

"The fox-trot isn't driving, so no."

"Don't worry, Knox." Her tone was the verbal equivalent of a pat on the head. "I'll get us there safely. You can be my navigator."

He grumbled. "Great."

"The Chekov to my Kirk."

"Come on," he said. "I'm Shatner. Everyone knows that."

She laughed. "No one knows that. Because it isn't true."

"Clearly I'm the captain of the starship *Enterprise*, Selena."

"O Captain! my Captain! I'm the one driving."

"Technically, as you are the one in red, I would be very concerned by the metaphor."

"This is going into serious nerd territory, Knox." She chuckled. "Do you remember we used to stay up all night with the old *Star Trek*, eating ice cream until we were sick when we were supposed to be having study group?"

"We studied," he said. "We all took it pretty seriously."

"Yeah," she said. "But at a certain point there was just no more retaining information, and we ended up vegging."

"Our college stories are pretty tame compared to some."

"Yeah," she said. "But I don't think you and I ever wanted to compromise our good standing at the university by smoking a lot of weed. We had to get out there and make our own futures. Away from our families."

"True," he returned.

"Which is why we are the successful ones. That's why we're the ones who have done so well."

He felt like he was falling into that great divide again. He wasn't sure what those words meant anymore. Hadn't been for some time. "I guess so."

Tough to think that he had spent all that time working like he had. Through school, and in business, only to reach existential crisis point by thirty-two. It was surprising. And a damn shame.

"Well," she said. "I think anyone who ever doubted us has been proved wrong. How about that?"

He shook his head, watching the familiar scenery fly by. It was so strange to be back here in Royal. He'd met Cassandra in Royal when visiting Will, and he'd decided he'd move there after college to be closer to her. They'd started their life here, their family.

He took it all in. The great green rolling hills and the strange twisty trees. So different from the mountainous terrain in Wyoming. So different from the jagged peaks that surrounded his ranch, which he'd always kept even during the time he'd lived in Royal. The ranch made him feel like he was closed in. Protected. In another place. In another world. Rather than back here where time seemed too harsh and real.

"True enough."

At least he had found a way to talk to Selena again. At least, they'd had a moment of connecting.

A moment where the weirdness of the kiss hadn't been the only thing between them. They had a history. She'd known him as a college kid, out of step with the privileged people he was surrounded by, determined to use that opportunity to make something of himself. She'd known him as a newlywed, a new father, a grieving man. A newly single man.

Selena was one of the most important people in his life.

"I know you think you're the captain," she said softly. "Just like I know you don't like tea."

A jolt went down his spine. "What?"

"You don't like tea."

"I…know. I didn't think you knew. You serve it to me all the time."

"And you never say anything."

"My mama would have slapped me upside the head," he said.

He didn't talk about her much, and for good reason, really. WillaMae McCoy was a hard, brittle woman who had definite ideas about right and wrong, until it came to the men she shacked up with and the bottle of liquor she liked best to dull the heartache of losing them.

"Really?" Selena asked.

"Yes. She was big on 'Yes, ma'am,' 'No, ma'am.' Good posture and holding the door open for a lady. And I certainly wouldn't have been allowed to turn down a cup of tea."

"Even if you didn't like it?"

He lifted a shoulder. "Manners."

"Well. Don't do that with me. You can always tell me."

Finally, they arrived at Will's family ranch, the place decked out for a big party. The lights were all on inside the house and he could make out a faint glow coming from behind the place.

And just as he had told Selena, most of the men were in jeans and button-up shirts, wearing white or black cowboy hats. It was Texas. There was no call to put on a tie. Though some of the men wore bolos.

"You okay?" he asked. Because lost in all the strangeness of the past few days, lost in the revelation that Will and Selena had married for reasons other than love, had been the fact that Will was her ex-husband. And it was possible that—even though they had actually gotten married for the trust fund— she was still hurt by the entire thing.

She hadn't said she wasn't, and she had spent all these years avoiding Will. Seeing as she'd gone to his funeral, she'd imagined she'd missed the chance to ever connect with him again.

But look how that had turned out.

"I'm fine," she said, forcing a smile. "It's a good thing," she said. "Getting to see Will. I'm glad that I got this chance."

"All right," he said.

Without thinking, he rounded to her side of the

car and opened the door for her, taking her hand and helping her out of the vehicle.

Then they walked into the party together. He placed his hand low on her back as he guided her through the front door of the massive ranch house. She whipped around to look at him, her eyes wide.

He removed his hand from her back. He hadn't even thought about it, how possessive a move it was. He had just done it. Because it had felt reasonable and right at the time.

He could tell by the expression on her face that it had actually been neither.

He stuffed his hand in his pocket.

The housekeeper greeted them and then ushered them out into the yard, where Cora Lee was waiting, greeting them with open arms and kisses on both cheeks.

When she pulled away, Knox had that sense again that she was the kind of woman you didn't want to cross. Sweet as pie, but there might be a razor blade buried in the filling.

Or at least, if there needed to be one, there would be.

"So good of you to come," she drawled.

"Of course," Selena said. "I'm just thrilled that Will is okay."

"So are we all, sugar," she said.

They moved back through the party and Selena shivered. He fought the urge to put his arm around her again. Obviously, she wasn't having that. Clearly, she was not open to him touching her. In spite of the fact that they had been friends for years.

It was that kiss.

And as he stood there, conscious of the newfound boundaries drawn in their relationship, he asked himself if he regretted that kiss.

No, sir. He sure as hell did not.

Because it had woken up some things inside of him he hadn't thought would ever wake up again.

And those thoughts put his mind back at the place it had been while he was getting ready for the party. He wasn't sure how he was going to move forward.

But maybe the desire for anonymous sex would come next.

He damn sure hoped so. Because relationships... Marriage. None of that was ever happening again.

And that, he realized, standing there in this crowded, loud Texas party with country music blaring over the speakers, was the real tragedy.

He had reached the point that so many people idealized. He had crawled out of the gutter, bloodied his knuckles getting there. He'd found love. He'd gotten married. He'd had a child.

And it had all come crashing down around him.

He knew what it looked like to achieve those things, and he knew what it looked like standing on the other side of losing them.

They were nothing but heartbreak and rubble.

He didn't want them again. He just couldn't do it.
He took a step away from Selena. He was not
going to touch her again. That much was certain.

Six

Selena felt Knox's withdrawal.

Although he had taken only a slight step to the side, she could sense that something had changed.

His eyes were distant. And he looked a lot more like the sad, wounded man she had first seen after his daughter's funeral than he looked like the friend she'd reminisced with in the car about their nerdy college life.

She started to say something, but he spotted someone they both knew from college and gave her a cursory hand gesture before walking away.

She felt deflated.

She knew she was acting a bit twitchy. But damn,

Knox looked handsome in that outfit. In those jeans that hugged his muscular thighs and ass. And that hard place between those muscular thighs that she had felt pressed up against her body just the other day.

The cowboy hat. Oh, the cowboy hat always made her swoon. Cowboys weren't her type. If they were, she would have her pick. She lived in Texas.

No, sadly *Knox* was her type. And that had always been her tragedy.

She was brooding, and pretty darned openly, too, when her friend Scarlett McKittrick spotted her from across the lawn and headed her way. Scarlett being Scarlett, she *bounded* across the lawn, her eyes sparkling with determination in the dim light. She was like a caffeinated pixie, which was generally what Selena liked about her, but also part of why she'd been avoiding Scarlett since Knox had come to town. She didn't want her friend to grill her on why he was hanging around, or to start asking questions about what was happening between them. She'd end up telling Scarlett everything and confessing she wanted Knox. She just didn't want to have that conversation.

It made her feel a little guilty since Scarlett's adoption of her son had just been finalized and she knew Scarlett might feel like the baby was why Selena wasn't hanging around as much. But that wasn't the reason. She and Scarlett had been friends for years, even though the bond wasn't as intense as the one

Selena shared with Knox, which was unsurprising, since Selena didn't secretly harbor fantasies about making out with Scarlett.

"Hi," Selena said, trying to sound bright.

"Hi, yourself," Scarlett said, her eyes assessing Selena in her overly perceptive manner. "I have escaped by myself for the evening, so I'm feeling good." She ran her hand through her short hair and grinned. "Thanks for asking."

"Sorry," Selena said. "I'm a terrible friend."

Scarlett waved a hand. "Yeah. A bit. But I'll live. What's happening with you and Knox?" The subject change nearly gave Selena whiplash.

"Nothing," Selena said, lying through her teeth.

"He seems... I mean, I haven't seen him *since*."

"I know," Selena said. "He's made himself scarce."

Scarlett bumped her with an elbow. "So have you recently."

"I'm sorry. I've been dealing with all the stuff with Will. And Knox came to stay at my house after the funeral that wasn't and he hasn't exactly left."

Scarlett's eyebrows shot up. "Really?"

"Yes," she said. "Don't go thinking weird ideas about it. There's nothing weird."

"If you say so. But he looked... He doesn't look good, Selena."

She took a deep breath of the warm night air, catching hints of whiskey and wildflowers, mingling with smoke from a campfire. "I know. He's not the same. But how could he be?"

"Yeah. I guess if he was, you'd be forced to think he was pretty callous. Or in denial."

Selena shook her head. "Well, I can say he's not in denial. He's pretty firmly rooted in reality."

Except for that kiss. That kiss had been a moment outside of reality. And it had been glorious.

"Anyway," Selena said, "he's feeling paranoid because of everything with Will. I mean, *someone* faked Will's death. And *someone* wanted me and everyone else at that memorial service. It's weird. And it is nice to have Knox here just in case anything goes down."

"Yeah. I questioned the wisdom of having a party tonight, even though the only people Cora Lee invited were those of us at the service when Will walked in. But also, it's Texas, and at least eight percent of the people here have a sidearm, so anyone who tried to cause trouble would end up on the wrong side of a shoot-out."

"No kidding."

"Hey," Scarlett said, obviously ready for a new topic. "When are you guys coming out to Paradise Farms? Or if you'd rather do something different, the ranch next door to mine is doing a thing where you can go glamping."

Selena blinked. "I'm sorry—what?"

"You know—" Scarlett waved her hand around "—*glamorous camping.*"

"I don't know anything about that. Mostly because I don't know anything about camping, Scarlett. As you well know."

"It's not like regular camping. Yes, you ride horses, and go on one of the long trails that takes two full days to complete, and there's an overnight checkpoint. But the food that's included is amazing and the tent that's set up is a really, really nice tent, luxurious even."

"I...I don't know." The idea of being alone with Knox on an abandoned trail, riding horses, sleeping under the stars—or under the canvas top of a very nice tent—all seemed a little bit...fraught. And by fraught, she meant it turned her on, which was probably a very bad thing considering their situation.

"Well, think about it. It'd be a great way to take a break from all the drama here in town. The invitation is open. Because it's new, the schedule is really vacant. And I know they'd be happy to have testimonials from both of you. You can come out to Paradise Farms and use my horses. Right now, people are bringing their own to ride the trail."

Selena tried to smile and not look like she was pondering Knox and close quarters too hard. "I'll think about it."

"Do that." Scarlett grinned. "And text me. I'm dying

at home buried under diapers and things. Babies are a lot of work."

"Okay. I promise."

Scarlett shifted. "Okay. Well, do text me. And… if anything…comes up. If you need to talk about *anything*. Please remember that you can call me."

"I will. Promise."

That left Selena standing alone as Scarlett went off to talk to someone else. She tapped her fingers together, and a passing waiter thrust a jar of what she assumed was moonshine into her empty hands.

She leaned forward, sniffing gingerly, then drew her head back, wrinkling her nose.

"I'm surprised you came."

She turned to see Will Sanders, her ex-husband— sort of. They hadn't spoken in so long it was weird to have him here next to her, talking to her. And it also made the years feel like they had melted away. Like there had been no fight. No stupid marriage. No accusations. Like greed and money—her greed—had never come between them.

"Yeah," she said, "fancy meeting you here. Especially since I thought you were dead."

"I would've thought you were pretty psyched about my demise, gingersnap."

"I've never understood that nickname. I'm not a redhead."

He winked, but it was different somehow than it had been. "No, but you're spicy with a bit of bite."

"Right. I guess I bit you a time or two." But not the way she'd bitten Knox. Not the way Knox thought she might have bitten Will. Her mind was terminally in a gutter right now.

"Yeah. But that's water under the bridge. A lot is thrown into perspective when you've been through what I have." She examined him for the first time. The hard line of his jaw, the slightly sharper glint to his eyes. He was not the same man he'd been. That much was certain. She could make out faint scarring on his face and wondered how much surgery he'd had to have to get himself put back together. She'd heard someone mention that Will had been in a boating accident in Mexico and left for dead. He'd been recovering and trying to make his way home all this time.

She wondered if there was anything that could put his soul back together.

"I'm sorry," she said. "And that was so easy to say it makes me seriously question why I didn't do it earlier."

"I know why you didn't do it earlier. Because you were angry. Because you were scared. It's fine, Selena. I'm not the kind of guy you need in your life anyway."

"Oh, I know," she said. "But it would be nice to be on speaking terms with you."

"I'm sorry if I hurt you," he said.

"You did not hurt me," she said, making a scoffing sound.

"I thought that was why you got so angry at me. Because you were in love with me."

In spite of herself, in spite of the absurdity of the situation, Selena let out a crack of laughter. "Will Sanders, you thought I was in love with you?"

"Yes."

"You are so full of it!" she all but exploded. And for some reason, she felt lighter than she had in days. Weeks. *Years.* "I was not in love with you."

"You asked me to marry you to help you get your trust fund. And then you got mad at me…"

"Because I thought our friendship was too good to be true, Will. I didn't have it the easiest growing up. I didn't have people in my life I could trust. I trusted you. And when Rich planted that seed of doubt…"

Everything in Will's body went hard like granite. Right down to his expression and the line of his mouth. "Right. Well. Rich has a lot to answer for."

"I just…" She tapped the side of the jar. "I wanted so badly to believe that what we had was real friendship. I guess maybe that wasn't super common for you with women, but it meant something to me."

"So—" he frowned "—you weren't in love with me?"

She laughed. "No."

"Then why did you ask me to marry you? You

could have just as easily asked Knox. Did I win a coin toss?"

Unbidden, her gaze drifted across the expanse of lawn, and her eyes found Knox. Effortlessly. Easily. Her eyes always went right to him.

"I see," he said, far too perceptive. Old Will would never have been so perceptive. "Well, this does make a few things clearer."

"I'm sorry I was such a terrible friend," she said. "I'm sorry I let my issues drive us apart. And I'm sorry I listened to Rich when you had never given me a reason to mistrust you. You would make a horrible gold digger, Will, and I see that now."

"Yeah, well, nothing like dying and coming back to life to make people think better of you," he commented. "Of course…the thing with my life at the moment is I can't have it back."

"What?"

"Someone has been living it for me, Selena. I didn't write you that letter. I didn't write letters to anyone."

"Will…" She stared at him, at the changes in his face. "What happened, Will?"

"Not talking about that yet," he said, his voice tight. "I don't know what's actually going on and until then…until then I'm just keeping watch on everything."

Silence settled between them, and Selena swallowed hard and nodded. "Well…well, I'm glad you're okay. And I'm really glad you're not dead."

Suddenly he smiled, and she thought she saw a glimpse of the Will she'd once known. "You know, when this is over I think I'm going to start a line of greeting cards. The Awkwardly Interrupted Funeral line. *So glad you're not dead. Hey, you rose from the grave and it's not even Easter.*"

"That sounds great," she responded, laughing.

Well, at least one relationship in her life wasn't a total mess.

"I have to make the rounds. As a reanimated corpse, I'm extremely popular." He stuffed his hands in his pockets and winked again. It seemed a little try hard at that point, but she could understand.

Will's life couldn't be totally normal at the moment, all things considered.

"Great," she said, a smile tugging at her lips.

She wrapped her arms around herself and looked at who was attending the party. She caught sight of Will's stepbrother Jesse Navarro, who was always a dark and sullen presence. Selena didn't know him personally, but she knew of him. She had moved to Royal after college, lured by Will's tales of it as some sort of promised land.

And it always had been for her. She'd found a sense of home here. Part of that was because at first she'd had Knox, since she and Will hadn't been on speaking terms. But even after Knox had left…

The town was special to her. Even if she was a latecomer.

She had seen Jesse at events before. Even without being a member of the Texas Cattleman's Club, it was impossible to move in the moneyed circles in Royal and not have some clue about who the people were in your age bracket.

She also saw the woman who'd had the child at Will's funeral. And she wondered if that was Will's baby. Wondered if she knew the truth about anyone.

Because the fact remained that if Will was the one responsible for all that heartbreak she'd been standing in the middle of at the funeral, as much as she might like him, he had a lot to answer for. A lot to atone for, now that he was back.

Suddenly, Jesse's gaze landed on that woman, and his eyes sizzled with heat.

Selena felt like she had to look away, like she was witnessing an intimate moment.

When she looked back, whatever connection she thought she'd spotted seemed to be gone. And the woman hadn't seemed to notice at all.

She looked around again, trying to get a visual on Knox, and saw that he was gone. Then she saw a figure standing just outside the lights on the lawn, holding a bottle of beer. She knew that was him. She knew him by silhouette. That wasn't problematic at all.

She ditched the moonshine in the jar and reached

for a bottle of her own beer, walking gingerly across the grass in her heels, making her way to where he was standing.

"Hi," she said.

He didn't jump. Didn't turn. As if he had already sensed her. That thought made the back of her neck prickle. Was he as aware of her as she was of him?

"Hi," he returned, lifting his bottle of beer to his lips. He took a long, slow pull. And she was grateful for the shroud of darkness. Because had it not been so dark, she would've watched the way his lips curved around the bottle, would have watched the way his Adam's apple moved as he swallowed the liquid.

And her whole body would have burned up. A lot like it was doing now, just imagining such things.

"I talked to Will," she said.

"Did you?" he asked, the words laden with a bite.

"I think we made amends, for what that's worth. It was something that needed to happen. There's a lot of stuff in my past, and I'm all bound up in it. No matter how successful I get, no matter how far I move forward, it's just there."

He lifted a shoulder. "I can relate to that."

Except she knew he was talking about something a lot more grave, and she felt instantly guilty.

"Why aren't you at the party? Don't you want to talk to Will?"

"I decided I wasn't really in a party mood once everything got going."

"All right." She wrapped her arms around herself to keep from wrapping her arms around him. "Do you want to leave?"

"That's fine. If you're having fun."

"I'm not sure I would call laying a ghost to rest fun. Just potentially necessary."

"Right."

Then she did reach out and touch him. Her fingertips brushed his shoulder, and she felt the contact down to her stomach, making it clench tight. "Knox."

His name was a whisper, a plea. But she didn't know what for. For normalcy? For an explosion?

His muscles tensed beneath her touch, and she felt like her stomach had been scooped out. Felt like she had been left hollow and wanting, aching for something that only he could give her.

She remembered what it felt like when his mouth pressed against hers. Finally, after all that time. She had kissed other men. Half-hearted attempts at finding a way she could be attracted to somebody who wasn't her best friend. It had never worked. It had never excited her.

This kiss haunted her dreams. It haunted her now.

She wanted to kiss him. She wanted to give him comfort. In any way she could. And they were out here in the darkness on the edge of this party. Where

Will Sanders had come back from the dead and everything was just freaking crazy.

So she decided to be crazy, too. She slid her hand upward to his neck, curving her fingers around his nape. And then she brought herself around to the front of him, placing her palm on his chest, directly over his heart, where it was raging hard and fast.

"Selena," he said, a word of warning. A warning she wasn't going to heed.

She stretched up on her tiptoes—because she was still too short to just kiss him, even in these heels—and a rush of pleasure flooded her, a rush of relief, the moment their mouths met.

She was lost in it. In the torrent of desire that overtook her completely as his scent, his flavor, flooded her senses.

It was *everything*. It was everything she remembered and more. Kissing him was like nothing else. It was like every fantasy colliding into one brilliant blinding firework.

Oh, how she wanted him. How she wanted this. She wrapped her arms around his neck, still clutching the bottle of beer tightly, and then he dropped his bottle, grabbing hold of her hips with both hands and tugging her heat against his muscular body. She could feel his arousal pressing against her stomach, and she wanted…she wanted to ride it.

She wanted to ride *him*.

"Please," she whispered.

She didn't know what she was begging for, only that if she didn't get it she would die.

He moved one hand down to her side, then down her lower hip around to the back of her knee. Then he lifted her leg and drew it up over his hip, opening her to that blunt masculine part of him.

She gasped and tilted her hips forward, groaning when a shot of pleasure worked its way through her body. She tilted forward, riding the wave of pleasure. Allowing herself to get caught up in this. In the rapturous glory of his mouth on hers, of his hard, incredible masculinity.

She would let him take her here, she realized. Let him strip her naked on the edges of this party and lay her down in the damp grass. Sweep her panties to the side and thrust inside of her, even though she'd never let another man do it before. She wasn't afraid. Not even remotely.

This was Knox McCoy and she trusted him with all that she was. Trusted him with her body.

I don't trust him. There's so much I haven't told him.

But if she told him everything, then he wouldn't look at her the same. What if he saw the same abused girl she always saw when she looked in the mirror, rather than the confident businesswoman she had become?

She couldn't stand for that to happen. She truly couldn't.

So maybe if there was this first. Maybe they could both find something in it. Something they needed.

He drew away from her, suddenly, sharply, his chest heaving with effort. She wished she could see his face. Wished she could read his expression. Then he slowly released his hold on her thigh, and she slid an inch or so down his body. Not the most elegant dismount, that was for sure. She was grateful for the darkness, because he couldn't see the fierce blush in her cheeks, couldn't get an accurate read on the full horror moving through her at the moment.

"I'm not sorry," she said, pulling her dress back into place.

"Did I ask you to be?" he bit out, his words hard.

"No," she said, "but you stopped."

"I stopped because I was close to fucking you right here at a party. Is that what you want?"

"I…" She was dizzy. She couldn't believe she was standing here listening to her friend say those words, directed at her. "That's a complicated question, Knox."

"No." He shook his head. "It's really not. Either you want to get fucked on the ground at a party by your best friend or you don't."

She looked away, feeling self-conscious even though she knew he couldn't see her expression. "Maybe not…on the ground…at a *party*."

"Selena," he said, gripping her chin, leaning forward and gazing at her with his dark, blazing eyes. "I can't give you anything. I can't give you anything other than sex."

"I didn't ask you for anything," she said, her voice small.

"We're friends. And that means I care about you. But I'm never, ever getting married again."

"It's kind of a long leap from fucking in the grass to a marriage proposal, don't you think, Knox?" she asked, self-protection making her snarky, because she needed something to put distance between them.

"I just meant this doesn't end anywhere but sex, baby. And I need our friendship. I haven't had a lot of bright spots in my life lately, and I hate to lose the one I have."

"But you want me," she said, not feeling at all awkward about laying that out there. Because he did. And she knew it.

"That doesn't mean having."

And then he just walked away. Walked away like they were in the middle of having a conversation. Like her heart wasn't still pounding so hard it was likely to go straight through her chest. Like she wasn't wet and aching for satisfaction that he had denied her, yet again.

And that was when she made a decision. She was going to have Knox McCoy. Because there was no going back now. They wanted each other. And she had been holding on to all those feelings for him for

"FAST FIVE" READER SURVEY

Your participation entitles you to:
✳ 4 Thank-You Gifts Worth Over $20!

Complete the survey in minutes.

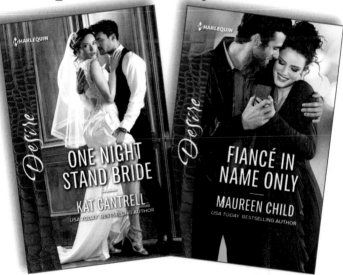

Get **2 FREE** Books

Your Thank-You Gifts include **2 FREE BOOKS** and **2 MYSTERY GIFTS**. There's no obligation to purchase anything!

See inside for details.

Dear Reader,

Since you are a lover of our books, your opinions are important to us... and so is your time.

That's why we made sure your **"FAST FIVE" READER SURVEY** can be completed in just a few minutes. Your answers to the five questions will help us remain at the forefront of women's fiction.

And, as a thank-you for participating, we'd like to send you **4 FREE THANK-YOU GIFTS!**

Enjoy your gifts with our appreciation,

Pam Powers

To get your
4 FREE THANK-YOU GIFTS:

✳ Quickly complete the "Fast Five" Reader Survey
and return the insert.

"FAST FIVE" READER SURVEY

1	Do you sometimes read a book a second or third time?	○ Yes ○ No
2	Do you often choose reading over other forms of entertainment such as television?	○ Yes ○ No
3	When you were a child, did someone regularly read aloud to you?	○ Yes ○ No
4	Do you sometimes take a book with you when you travel outside the home?	○ Yes ○ No
5	In addition to books, do you regularly read newspapers and magazines?	○ Yes ○ No

YES! I have completed the above Reader Survey. Please send me my 4 FREE GIFTS (gifts worth over $20 retail). I understand that I am under no obligation to buy anything, as explained on the back of this card.

225/326 HDL GMVP

FIRST NAME   LAST NAME

ADDRESS

APT.#   CITY

STATE/PROV.   ZIP/POSTAL CODE

READER SERVICE—Here's how it works:

so long that she knew a couple of things for certain. They weren't going away, and no man could take his place as it was.

She had known a lot of girls in college who had thought they needed to get certain guys out of their systems, which had always seemed to her a fancy way to excuse having sex when you wanted it, even though you knew it was a really bad idea and the guy was never going to call. It had always ended in sadness, as far as she had seen.

But Knox had been in her system for so long, and there was no other way he was getting out of it. She knew that. This wasn't a guy she had met in class a few weeks ago, a guy she had exchanged numbers with at a party.

She had known Knox for the better part of her adult life and she wasn't just going to wake up one morning and not want him.

So maybe this was the way forward.

She pulled her phone out, still not ready to go back to the party, to go back into the lights where people might see her emotional state. Where they might be able to read what had just happened. And she texted Scarlett.

So, about that glamping.

Seven

Knox had stuck it out at the party just to be a stubborn cuss. By the time he and Selena got back in the car and started to drive to the ranch, he expected her to unleash hell on him.

Instead, she didn't. Instead, she was silent the entire way, and he didn't like that. He didn't like it at all. He'd enough of hard, sad silences. He preferred to be screamed at, frankly. But Selena didn't seem to be in the mood to give him what he wanted.

And he said nothing.

Then when they pulled in the driveway and finally got out, heading into the house, she spoke.

"We're going glamping tomorrow," she said, her expression neutral, but vaguely mischievous.

"What?"

"Scarlett suggested it. We're going on a trail ride. And we are staying overnight in a luxury tent."

"I was going to head back to Jackson Hole," he said, lying, because he had no plans to do that at all. And for the first time, he questioned why.

He didn't like that all these interactions with Selena forced him to do things like ponder his motivations.

"I don't care. Change your ticket. You're rich as God, Knox. It's not like it's a problem."

"No," he said slowly.

"You're coming glamping with me, because you're still not okay, I'm clearly not okay, and we need to do something to get back on track. We are not leaving our friendship here. You are not going off to Wyoming for however the hell long and not seeing me. Because it's going to turn into not seeing me for months, for years, as we avoid all the weirdness that has sprung up between us."

Oh, he was personally all right with avoiding the weirdness. But obviously, she wasn't.

"Okay," he found himself agreeing, and he couldn't quite fathom why.

"It'll be fun," she said, grinning at him, all teeth. And it made him damn suspicious.

"I'm not overly familiar with fun," he said, purposefully making his tone grave.

"Well," she said, "this will be."

He had his doubts, but he also knew Selena Jacobs on a mission was not a creature to be trifled with. And not one easily derailed.

So they would go on a trail ride. They would go camping.

Once upon a time he'd liked to ride, he'd liked to camp. Why the hell not?

Maybe she was right. Maybe it would remind him of some of the things he used to like.

Although, privately, he feared that it would go much the same way as the party had gone. That all it would do was reinforce the fact that he couldn't enjoy things the way he used to. That he had nothing left to look forward to in his life.

Because he couldn't think of a single dream he hadn't achieved. Then two of them he lost. And one of them just didn't mean a thing without the others.

And he had no idea where the hell you went from there.

Camping, it seemed.

He shook his head and followed Selena into the house.

By the time they were saddled up and ready to ride, Selena was starting to have some doubts. But not enough to turn back.

They were given a map and detailed instructions on how the trail ride would work, and then she and Knox were sent off into the Texas wilderness together. Alone, except for each other.

And the condoms Selena had stuck in her bag.

Because this was a seduction mission more than it was anything else, and she was completely ready to go there.

Well, except for the nerves. And the doubts. There were those. But that was all virgin stuff.

Oh, and the fact that she was going to see her best friend's penis.

The thought made her simultaneously want to giggle and squeeze her thighs together to quell the ache there.

Her cheeks heated as she realized the rhythm of the horse's gait did a little something for it. Her face flamed, her whole body getting warm.

Knox McCoy had turned her into a sex-crazed pervert. And they hadn't even had sex yet.

He might not want to have sex with me.

Yes, that was the risk. She might get Knox alone in a tent, around a romantic campfire, and she might strip herself completely naked and get denied. It was possible. It was not a possibility she was hoping for. But it might happen. The idea did not thrill her.

But there was no great achievement without great risk. And anyway, if there was one thing she had kind of learned from this whole experience with

Will's death-that-was-not-actually-a-death, it was that time was finite.

She had stood at Will's funeral and had regretted leaving things bad between them. She didn't want to regret Knox.

Somewhere in the back of her mind she knew that if this ruined her friendship with Knox she was going to regret that. She was going to regret it a whole hell of a lot. But at least she wouldn't wonder. Right now, it seemed worth the risk.

Maybe on the other side it wouldn't. But she wasn't on the other side yet.

She squared her shoulders and they continued to ride down the trail.

It was beautiful. The land was sparse, filled with scrub brush and twisty, gnarled trees that were green in defiance to their surroundings. She had been told that the trail would wind toward some water, and that it would get shadier and greener there, which was why it was good to do this leg early in the morning, before the sun rose high in the sky and the heat and humidity started to get oppressive.

But the view around her wasn't her primary reason for being here, anyway. It was him. It was Knox.

"So," she said, "it's nice out."

"Yeah," he responded, taciturn like he had been last night.

It was funny, how she had gone from the one

being all angry about the kiss to him being all angry. What a delight.

She hoped that banging him was slightly more delightful.

The thought made her nerves twitch.

"So, how many hours is it to camp?" he asked.

"About six," she said.

"That seems a little bit crazy," he responded.

"I know," she said, and then she frowned. Because she hadn't really considered that. The fact that she was going to launch a full-out seduction after having been on the back of a horse all day. Honestly, there was a sweat situation that might be problematic. Not that she minded if he was sweaty. She was all okay with that. It was pheromones or something. She had always liked the way Knox smelled when he'd been sweating. After he had gone for a run in college and he would come back to hang at her dorm for a while, steal some food off her and her roommate. He had walked by her, and her stomach would go into a free fall.

It was so funny, how she had buried that reaction down deep, and how it was all coming up now. Bringing itself into the light, really.

She had been in full denial of her feelings for him for so long. While she had definitely known they were there, she didn't focus on them. But now she was admitting everything to herself. That she was a sucker for the way he smelled. That his voice skimmed over her skin like a touch. That in so many ways she had been waiting for him. Waiting for this. And that excuses about how busy she was, how important the company was, were not really the reasons why she didn't date.

It was because no man was Knox, and never would be.

As she made idle chatter for the rest of the ride, she fought against cloying terror. She was headed toward what was her undeniable destiny and almost certain heartbreak.

But she'd come too far to turn back now. She simply couldn't.

Eventually, they did come to that river, and they found themselves beneath the canopy of trees as the sun rose high in the sky. They arrived at camp before the sun began to set, a glorious, serene tent out in the middle of nowhere right next to the river.

There were Texas bluebells in the grass that surrounded it. A little oasis just for them. There was a fire pit, places to sit. It really was the most civilized camping she had ever seen.

"I am going to jump in the river," Knox said. He got off the horse and stripped his shirt off over his head.

And she froze. Just absolutely froze as the shirt's fabric slowly rolled up over his torso and revealed his body.

Lord, what a body.

"What?" he asked.

Well, great. She'd been caught staring openly. At her friend's half-naked body. Talk about telegraphing her seduction plans.

"Nothing." She blinked. "I'll go… We can get the horses settled and then I'll get my swimsuit."

But her gaze was fully fixed on his broad, bare chest. On all those fantastic, perfect muscles. Which she had felt through his shirt a time or two in the past few days. But now… Seeing it like that, dusted with just the right amount of pale hair, glistening with sweat… She wanted to lick him.

She imagined the rules of friendship generally prevented that. But she was fully violating those anyway, so she was just going to embrace the feeling.

"Come on," he said, nodding once. "Let's get the horses into the corral."

She went through the motions of leading the horses into the gated area and making sure there was fresh water in the trough, but really, she was just watching Knox.

The way the sun glinted on his golden hair and highlighted the scruff on his face—she wanted so badly to run her fingers over it. The way the muscles in his forearms went taut as he removed the horses' bridles and saddles…

He bent down low, setting about cleaning their

hooves, his body putting on a glorious play of strength and sculpted masculinity that took her breath away.

He was such a familiar sight. But in context with desire, with what she wanted to have happen later, he was like a stranger. And that both thrilled and excited her.

When they finished taking care of the animals, he straightened, and she was momentarily struck dumb again by his beauty. It was a wonder she'd ever managed to get to know the guy. His looks were a serious barrier to her ability to form cogent thoughts and words that were more than noises.

"Why don't you go on in and get your suit?" he asked, handing her her pack.

His fingers brushed against hers and she felt the touch like a bolt of lightning. All the way through her body.

Selena scurried into the tent, barely able to take in the glory of it. There was an actual bed inside, seating, a woodstove, all surrounded by beautifully draped canvas. The bed was covered in furs and other soft, sumptuous things. It was the perfect place to make love to a man you had been fantasizing about all of your life.

And when darkness fell, she was going to do just that.

The corners of her lips turned upward when she realized there was only one bed in the place. And she wondered if Scarlett was matchmaking. If Selena had been that damned transparent. She changed quickly into a black bikini, ignoring the moment of wishing it covered more of her body, and headed outside.

She was gratified when Knox's expression took on that similar "hit with a shovel" quality she had been pretty sure her own had possessed a few moments ago when he had stripped off his shirt.

"Nice suit," he said.

He was wearing a pair of swim shorts that she wondered if he'd been wearing beneath everything else the whole time. Or if he had just quickly gotten naked outside.

And then she thought way too long and hard about that.

"Thank you," she said.

The shorts rode low, revealing every sculpted line just above that part of him that was still a mystery to her. She was doing her best not to look like a guppy spit out onto the shore. Gaping and gasping. She had a feeling she was only semi-successful.

"There's only one bed," she commented. "I didn't realize that."

As if that mattered. She was planning to seduce him anyway.

"Oh," he said. "Well, I can sleep on the floor."

"Let's worry about that later," she said, because she hoped that both of them would be completely all right with the fact that there was only one bed just a little bit later.

They went down toward the river, and in spite of the heat, when she stuck her toe in the slow-moving water, she shuddered slightly.

"Oh, come on," he said. "It's not that cold."

As if to demonstrate all of his masculine bravado, he went straight into the water, wading in up to his hips and then lying flat on his stomach and paddling out toward the center of the wide body of water.

She took a deep breath and followed suit, screeching as the water made contact with the tender skin on her stomach. "It is cold," she shouted at him.

"You're a baby," he responded, turning over onto his back and paddling away from her.

"I am not a baby," she said. She swam toward him and then splashed at him. He laughed, reaching out and grabbing her wrist, drawing her against him. She didn't know what the intent had been. Maybe to stop her from splashing him, but suddenly, her legs were all tangled up with his and her breasts were pressed against his bare chest. The wet swimsuit fabric did absolutely nothing to provide a barrier between them. Her nipples were hard, sensitive, partly from the chill of the water and partly just from him. From her desire for him.

"Knox," she said. "If you don't like it, tell me. I don't want to be tea."

"You're not tea," he said.

"Good. I'd hate for you to sleep with me because of good manners. A girl wants to be wanted."

And something in his eyes changed. His jaw was tight, the lines by his mouth drawn, deep. And she could see the struggle there. The fight.

"I don't need forever," she said. Her seduction plan had just gone out the window. This electricity between them was sparking right now. And she was going to make the most of it. She was going to take it. "I just need you. For a little while. I've wanted you... Always. I have. This isn't new for me. And it's not going away." She raised her hands, trusting him, trusting his strong, steady hold to keep her afloat. She traced those deep lines on either side of his lips with her thumbs, stroking him. Touching him the way she had always dreamed about touching him. Freely, without holding back.

That was the sad thing. She felt a whole hell of a lot for him, and yet she'd always, always held it back, held back a part of herself.

She was tired of that. And she was surrounded by reminders of why it was wrong. Time wasn't infinite. She'd thought she'd missed a chance to apologize to Will.

She wasn't going to miss this chance.

"You want this?" he asked, his voice rough. "You want me right now? Let me tell you, Selena, all I can give you is selfish. I haven't had sex in two years. A little bit more, maybe. Because it's not like there was a whole lot going on during the divorce. During the grief. And I...I don't have any control left in me. I wanted to do the right thing. I wanted to be honest with you about what I could and couldn't give you, but if you keep offering it to me…"

"If I keep offering it to you then you need to trust me." She met his gaze and held it. Tried to ignore her breathlessness, her nerves. "I'm your friend. I've been your friend for a long time. Haven't I always taken what you've given to me? Haven't we always been there for each other? That's what this is. I want to be there for you. And I want this, too. This isn't pity sex, Knox. I want it. I want you. I think you want me. So let's… Let's just trust that we'll find our way. Because we are friends. We've been through hell together. It wasn't my hell, Knox, but I walked alongside you. Trust me. Trust me to keep walking with you."

She was on the verge of tears, emotion clogging her throat, and crying wasn't what she wanted. It wasn't what this was supposed to be. It was supposed to be physical, and it was becoming emotional. But too late she realized, as she clung to him while he treaded water for them both, with Knox it was never going to be anything but emotional. Because they cared for each other.

And emotion was never going to stay outside of the sex. It was never going to be sex in one column and friendship in the other. They were bringing sex into a friendship. And that was big and scary, and not something she could turn away from.

"Trust me," she said, a final plea before he closed the distance between them.

Eight

Knox had known he was lost the moment she had come out of the tent wearing that bikini. He hadn't even given himself a chance. When he had grabbed hold of her in the water… It hadn't been to stop her from splashing him. It had simply been because he couldn't stand to not touch her anymore. He had to do it. He'd had to bring her against his body. Because he couldn't stand to not have his hands on her.

And as he held her he had the fleeting concern that this was going to be the most selfish sex on the face of the planet, and he was going to treat his best friend to it. She didn't deserve that. She deserved more. She deserved better. But he didn't have control. Not anymore.

He was a man stripped of everything. Life had simply stolen every fucking thing from him in the last two years. He couldn't fight this. Not with what he had left.

He just wanted. And he was so tired of wanting. There were so many things he couldn't have. He could not have Eleanor back, no matter how much he wanted her.

He couldn't fight death. No matter how he wanted to. How he wished that there was a sword he could have picked up so he could do battle with death. Instead, he'd had to stand by helplessly, not able to do a damn thing. For a man who had never accepted the limits of life, losing to death with such resounding finality had been incomprehensible.

But he could have this. He could have Selena.

He didn't have to fight it, and he damn sure wasn't going to. Not anymore.

So he kissed her. He kissed her like he was drowning in this river and she was the air. He kissed her like there wasn't going to be anything after it. Because for all he knew, there wouldn't be. Life was a bitch. A cruel, evil bitch who took as much as she gave, so he was going to take something of his own.

Maybe anger at the world wasn't the way to approach a seduction. Maybe it wasn't the way to engage with his best friend, but he couldn't help himself.

Couldn't do anything but lean into it. Lean into her. When she parted her lips and slid her tongue against his, he forgot to keep kicking, and they sank slightly beneath the water, the surface slipping past their shoulders. "We need to get out of here," he said, paddling them both toward the shore.

"There's that bed," she said softly, stroking her hand over his face, over his shoulders, the slide of skin against skin slick from the water.

He looked into her dark eyes to get a read on what she was thinking. "Did you plan this?"

"No," she said, looking very much like the picture of pristine innocence. In a black bikini that looked like sin.

"You didn't." Her eyes sparked with a little bit of heat, and a lot of the stubbornness he thought was cute about Selena at the best of times. It was cuter now, considering he was holding her nearly naked curves.

"Well." Her smile turned impish. "I didn't know there would be one bed. But I did know that I wanted you. And I figured this was as good a way as any to go about having you."

"Minx," he said, kissing her again. Kissing her until they were both breathless, out there in the bleached Texas sun.

Then he swept her up and carried her back toward that tent.

He didn't bother to dry either of them off when

he deposited her on the plush bed at the far side of the canvas wall. He stood there, looking at every delicious inch of her. Those full breasts, barely contained by the swimsuit top, her small waist and firm stomach. Those hips. Wide and delicious, and her thighs, which were full and lovely. Shaped like a delicious pear he definitely wanted to take a bite out of.

He pushed his wet shorts down his thighs, careful with his straining arousal. And it was gratifying to watch her mouth drop open, to watch her eyes go wide.

She squeezed her thighs together, drawing one leg up slightly, biting her lip.

"See something you like?" he asked.

She nodded. "Yeah," she said. And it was rare for Selena to not have a snarky comment follow.

"Do you want this?" he asked.

"Yes," she said, the word breathless. "I want it so much." She rolled to her side, her wet hair falling over her shoulder, her eyes wide. "Don't change your mind."

He glanced down at his extremely prominent erection. "Oh, I'm not in a position to change my mind. Or to do much of anything with my mind at the moment, especially thinking."

She settled back into the blankets, looking satisfied with that statement. "I'm okay with that."

He got onto the bed, moving over her, kissing her again, reaching behind her neck and undoing the tie on her bikini top in one fluid motion. Then he did the other one, taking the wet cups away from her breasts.

His breath caught in his throat as he looked at her. At that glorious, golden skin, her tight, honey-colored nipples.

He leaned forward, flicking the tip of one sensitive bud with his tongue, gratified when she gasped and arched against him. He sucked her deep into his mouth, lost completely in his own desire. His need to feast on her, to gorge himself on her beauty.

He wasn't thinking about anything in the past. Wasn't thinking about anything but this. But her. There was no room for anything but desire inside of him. There was nothing else at all.

He smoothed his hands down her narrow waist to those full hips, gripped her bikini bottoms and tugged them down her legs. And he groaned when he saw that dark thatch of curls at the apex of her thighs. He kissed her stomach, all the way down low to that tender skin beneath her belly button. Then he forced her legs apart, his cock pulsing, his stomach muscles getting impossibly tight as he looked at his friend like this for the first time. He felt her try to close her legs, try to move away from him.

He wasn't going to let her get away with that.

She might have orchestrated this little camping trip. Might have thought she could conduct a seduction. And he was seduced; there was no doubt about that. But she wasn't in charge. Not now. Hell no.

He leaned forward, breathing in the scent of her. Musk and female and everything he craved. His mouth watered, and he leaned forward, sliding his tongue over her slick flesh, flicking that sweet little clit with the tip of his tongue. She gasped, her hips bucking off the bed, simultaneously moving toward him and away from him. He held her fast, grabbing hold of both hips, drawing her roughly against his mouth where he could have his fill and maintain control of the movements.

She tried to twist and ride beneath him, but he held her fast, pleasuring her with his lips and his tongue, pressing his fingers deep inside of her until she cried out, until her internal muscles pulsed around him.

"Knox," she said, his name thin and shaky on her lips, her entire body boneless. And that satisfied him. Because it had been a long damn time since he'd had a woman, and there was a deep satisfaction to making her come that he couldn't even describe.

He could do that to her body. This need, this skill existed inside of him, and the desire to practice it was there. He'd left that need boxed up inside of him for years. In a stack in the corner of his soul. Anything that wasn't work, anything that wasn't breathing.

Right now, this felt like breathing. And he didn't simply feel alive. He felt like Knox.

He wanted to do it again. Again and again. He wanted to make her scream his name. But she was reaching for him, urging him up her body, urging him to kiss her again. Who was he to deny her?

He was going to give her everything.

Everything he had.

He settled between her thighs, kissing her deeply. He wanted this to last longer. Wanted to go on. But he just didn't possess the control. He needed to be inside of her. And he needed it now. He could only take so much satisfaction from her orgasm without desperately needing his own.

He pressed the head of his cock to the entrance of her body, found her wet and ready for him. Then he slid himself upward, drawing his length over those slick folds, teasing her a little before moving back to her entrance and thrusting in hard.

Then he froze as she tensed beneath him. As she let out a cry that had nothing at all to do with pleasure.

Somehow, Selena was a virgin.

Selena tried *so* hard not to be a baby when the sharp, tearing pain moved through her. He had just made her feel so good. And really, she wanted this. She wanted him. But the invasion of his body into hers hurt and she hadn't been able to keep back the cry of shock when he had entered her.

Screaming in pain was probably not the best move on her part. A pretty surefire way to kill the mood. Knox froze, looking down at her with anger written all over his handsome face.

She felt him start to move away from her, felt his muscles tense as he prepared to pull back. So he could stop touching her. So he could run out into the desert in the late afternoon and take his chances with the sun and snakes rather than with her. But she didn't want him to go.

So she clung to him, desperation probably leaving marks behind on his skin, digging her nails into his shoulders and kissing him fiercely, rocking her hips against his, ignoring the pain. She didn't want him to stop. It was too late anyway. Her virginity was gone. The hard part, the scary part, was over.

She didn't want to stop. Not now.

He tried to pull away again but she moved her hands down, clapping them over his muscular ass and holding him to her. She shook her head, her lips still fused to his.

He said nothing. Then he just continued on, slowly withdrawing from her body before thrusting back inside. He shuddered, lowering his head, his forehead pressed to hers. And she recognized the moment where whatever reservations he'd had were washed away by his own tide of need.

She'd had an orgasm already; he had not.

"Yes," she whispered as he began to move inside of her. As he began to establish a steady, luxurious rhythm that erased the pain she had felt only a moment before.

She wrapped her legs around his narrow hips, urging him on, chasing the pleasure she had felt before. And it began to build, low and deep inside of her, a band of tension that increased in intensity, drawing her closer to a second release. But this one seemed to come from somewhere deeper.

This time, when she shattered, it was just as he did, as his muscles tensed and his body shuddered, as his own orgasm washed through her, his thick, heavy cock pulsing as he spilled himself into her.

And when it was over, they lay there gasping, and she knew she was never going to be the same again. That there was no getting anyone out of her system. That her need for him would never change.

But along with that realization came a deep sense of peace. One that she was sure would vanish. But for now, she clung to it. For now, she clung to it and him, because reality would hit soon enough.

And she was in no hurry.

Because she had a feeling as soon as the afterglow receded there would be questions. She had a feeling there were in fact going to be quite a few follow-up questions. And what she really hadn't thought through in this moment was that there were going to be a lot of questions about Will.

She closed her eyes. Of course, she had already alluded to the fact that their marriage wasn't everything it seemed. So maybe Knox wouldn't be completely shocked. Maybe.

Well, even if he was—maybe that wasn't the end of the world. Maybe it was time to share the truth with him. She had closed him off. And now... Now he had been inside her body. So maybe that time was over. Maybe she just needed to go for it.

There was only one way to find out.

"Yes," she said, finding courage from deep inside that she hadn't realized existed. "I was a virgin."

He swore and moved away from her. She looked over at him just in time to see him scrubbing his hands over his face in what one might be forgiven for assuming was despair.

She folded her hands and rested them on her bare stomach, staring up at the canvas ceiling. "I assume you have queries."

"Yes," he responded. "I have several."

"Well," she said. "My marriage to Will wasn't real. I mean, we were never in a relationship."

"Never?" He treated her to a long hard look.

"No," she said. "We were never in a relationship at all. It was purely to help me get the trust-fund money."

"Why didn't you come to me? You could have

picked either of your friends to help you out with this and you asked him?"

Panic fluttered in her breast and she took a deep breath, trying to tap it down. She wasn't going to tell him that she hadn't asked because she couldn't face the possibility that living with him wouldn't have felt fake to her. She wasn't going to bring up her feelings at all. "I just... Look what happened with my friendship with Will afterward. Don't tell me I was wrong in trying to protect our friendship from problems like that. Choosing Will seemed necessary. Marrying him seemed like the only thing I could do to make sure that you and I were going to be okay. You were always more important to me, Knox. I just didn't..."

"That's bullshit, Selena," he said. "I know it is. Give me a straight answer."

"Why?" she asked. "I don't want to give you a straight answer. Because there is no good answer."

"I want the truth."

"Fine," she said. "I was afraid we would end up like this." She swept her arm up and down, indicating their nudity. "I didn't worry about that with Will. Not at all. It was just never like that between us. I never had those feelings for him."

"You had them for me."

"Yes," she said. "That's kind of obvious, considering we are lying here naked."

"But even back then?" he asked.

He'd already confessed to being attracted to her, but she hadn't handed out a similar confession. For her it felt so raw. So deep.

"I wanted you. But I knew I wasn't in a position to have you. I thought maybe someday... And then... marrying Will was a bad choice, Knox. And it's one I've never been particularly interested in interrogating. It ruined a lot of things."

"About the time you got divorced I was with Cassandra."

"Yes," she said. "In a lot of ways, I was grateful for that. Because it helped us preserve our friendship. I don't regret that neither of us made a move. I feel like it was actually better. I feel like if it had happened when we were young, we wouldn't have been able to...process this. We wouldn't have been able to separate the attraction from the friendship."

"And you think we can now?"

"I think we're both tired," she said, obviously. "I think we're both fatigued after spending a long time denying what we wanted. It's a pattern. In both of our lives. I'm not going to pretend to compare my struggle to yours. I'm really not. But...why fight this? We both wanted it. And for the first time, we're in a place where we can both take it. It was always wrong, and maybe in the future it will be wrong again. Maybe it will just naturally fade away."

"Is that what you really believe?"

"Yes," she said. "I do. I believe this is something we can work out. This is something we can have."

"But… Hell, Selena," he said. "You've really never been with another guy?"

"No. I was really busy. I was really busy growing the company and…"

"Yeah, usually that's the kind of thing people say when they miss a lot of coffee dates. Not when they just kind of forgot to have sex ever."

Now this, she could not be honest about. She was not going to have a discussion with him about how no man had ever seemed to measure up to him in her mind.

Because that was beyond sad.

"It really wasn't something that mattered to me. And then… Over the past few weeks with you…" She cleared her throat. "I'm attracted to you. I always have been. But it's not something I dwell on. I mean, you were married to somebody else. You had another life. And I always respected that. I did. What you had with Cassandra… I would never have dreamed of encroaching on it. I care about you like a friend, and I kind of want to tear your clothes off and bite you like a crazed lioness, and those two things are separate. But there was never any crazed lioness fantasies while you were married." That was a little lie. There was the occasional fantasy, but she had known she could never act on it.

He paused for a moment, then placed his hand on her. "So your attraction went dormant?"

"Yes," she said. "Your marriage was the winter of our attraction. It hibernated."

"Your libido hibernated," he said, his tone bland.

"Yeah," she said. "And my burrow was work. Work and friends and establishing my life in Royal." She let out a heavy sigh. "I never wanted to get married and have a family," she admitted. "My father was… You know he was difficult. And it's…" She knew it was time to share everything. They were naked, after all. They were naked and he had just taken her virginity, and there really were very few secrets left between them. But the last one was hers. She was holding it. She had to give it up.

"My father used to beat us. He was violent. His temper was unpredictable. We walked like there was broken glass under our feet all the time. Doing the very best we could not to bring that temper up. It was terrible. Terrifying. I will never, ever submit myself to that kind of thing again."

"So is that why you avoided relationships?"

"I would say that's why they weren't a priority. I'm not sure that I avoided them. I just didn't pursue them."

"You're being difficult."

"Yeah, well," she said. "I reserve the right to be difficult. I *can* be difficult now. That's the beauty of life on your own terms."

"And you think that's the key to happiness?" he asked, brushing his knuckles idly over her hip. It was a question void of judgment, but it made her chest feel weird all the same. Mostly because she'd never thought of it in those terms.

"It's a luxury. One that I appreciate. That's why I was so desperate to marry Will," she said. "Because I needed that money. Because I needed to be able to control my life. Because if I couldn't, then I was always going to be under my father's thumb."

"He *hit* you?" he asked.

"Yes," she said. "All the time. For anything. For attitude, disrespect. For not complying with his wishes when he wanted us to. We didn't have any control. We had to be the perfect family. His perfect wife. His perfect daughter. He didn't want me to go to college. He didn't want me to have any kind of autonomy at all. My grandfather is the one who helped me enroll in Harvard. But then he died. And I knew I wasn't going to find any more support. I wasn't going to have the resources for college. I was going to have to go back home, Knox, and I couldn't face that. I didn't want to need my father again. Ever. And I needed to get my hands on that trust fund in order to make that happen. In order to protect myself. To protect my mother. After I got it, I moved her out of the house. I installed her somewhere he couldn't get to her. I did everything I could do with my money to make sure we were never beholden to him again."

He shifted, tightening his hold on her. "I didn't know it was that bad." His words were like ground glass, sharp and gritty, and it gratified her to know that Knox was holding her tight with murder on his mind, because he couldn't stand the thought of her being hurt.

She was right to trust him.

"We all have our own struggles," she said, working to keep her tone casual. "I never wanted anyone to look at me like I was broken. Like I needed to be treated gently. I've always felt strong. Growing up that way, I had to be. But I protect what I have. I protect what's mine.

"You can see how our relationship, love, all of that never figured into my plans. I could never see myself submitting to a man controlling my life. To anyone controlling my life. To love controlling my life. Because that was my experience. It took so much for my mother to leave because she loved him, not just because she was afraid of him. Because part of her wanted to make it work. Wanted to find the man she had once known. The one who had made her fall for him in the first place. No matter how much I tried to tell her that man never existed, it was difficult for her to accept."

Selena took a deep breath before continuing, "She refused to press charges in the end. She used to cry. And say that I ruined her life by breaking up the marriage. By sending her to live in Manhattan, far away from him, and safely ensconced in an apartment there. She would think about going back to him, and it was only her fear that kept her away. She skips therapy all the time, no matter how many appointments I set up. I just... I never wanted to be that creature. Ever."

Knox grabbed hold of her chin, met her gaze. "You never could be."

She reached up, curled her fingers over his wrist and held his arm steady. "Any of us can be. At least, that's what I think. One step in the wrong direction and you're on that path, and at some point you're too many steps in, and you can't imagine going back. I've never thought I was above anything. I've never thought I was too good, too smart... Because that's not it. That's not what does it. We can all get bound up in it."

He looked genuinely stricken by that. "I never thought of it like that," he admitted.

"I know. It's human nature to want to believe people are at fault for their own bad situations. And often times they are complicit. But I don't think it was a fundamental personality flaw that made my mother stay with my father. It was fear of change. A fear of losing what she had. Because what if she ended up with less?"

"But she stayed in a house with a man who hit her daughter. You might be able to excuse that, Selena, but I don't think I can."

She looked away from him. "Sometimes I have a hard time with that. I won't lie to you. I can't have a relationship with my father. He's not a good man. He hurt me. He hurt my mother. He was made of rage that had nothing to do with us. I'm convinced it had everything to do with some kind of anger at himself. But whatever it was, it's nothing I want touching my life. So yes. I feel like I could be angry at her. Maybe I would even be justified. Because you're right. She did stay. Her fear was bigger than her desire to take action to get us out. In the end, my fear of living in that hell forever is what made me take action. And I just... We are out. And I don't have the energy for anger anymore. I want to have at least one relationship with one family member that isn't toxic. I want to heal what I can."

"That's pretty damned big of you," he said.

She laughed, lifting her shoulder. "Sure, but then, I also don't want to have a romantic relationship, so I'm emotionally scarred in other ways."

"I can appreciate that."

Silence fell over them and she allowed herself to fully take in the moment. The fact that she was lying there, skin to skin with her best friend. With the man she had fantasized about all of her life. She had told him everything. She had finally laid bare all the secrets she had been so scared to roll out. But on the heels of sharing everything came the revelation she had been working on avoiding. The real reason she had been afraid of confiding in him all this time.

It wasn't just that she cared for him. It wasn't just that she was attracted to him. She was in love with Knox McCoy, and she always had been. In love with a man she could never allow herself to have, because she had sworn that she would never get involved in those kinds of relationships.

And she was such a fool. Because she had been in love with him from the moment he had first walked into her life. She had thought she could keep him as a friend, and ignore the bigger feelings, the deeper feelings, but that was a lie. There was no avoiding it. There never had been.

But she didn't tell him that. She had let out all her other secrets and replaced them with another. One that she hoped he would never discover.

Because as horrifying as it was to admit to herself that she was in love with him, it would be even worse to have him know and have him reject her.

So she laid her head on his chest and focused on the rhythm of his heartbeat, on the way his skin felt beneath hers.

It wasn't love. But for now, maybe it was enough.

Nine

They finished out the trail ride the next day in relative silence. Knox was saddle sore, because it had been a while since he had ridden a horse. And it had been a while since he had ridden a woman. But he and Selena had definitely indulged themselves the entire night. He still wasn't sure what to make of any of it. Of the fact that he'd made love to his best friend, of the fact that she had been a virgin.

Yeah, he didn't even the hell know. But things weren't terribly awkward, which was a miracle in and of itself.

When they arrived back at Paradise Farms he noticed that Selena was pretty cagey with Scarlett as they deposited the horses and thanked her for the generous loan.

"She knew, didn't she?" Selena asked when they got back into the car and headed down the highway.

"Do you think so?"

"Well, I wonder, because she obviously knew the tent only had one bed."

He chuckled. "So you think she was trying to set you up?"

"I think she was trying to set *you* up," she said. "She thought you seemed sad."

"I am," he responded, his tone dry. The answer more revealing than he'd intended it to be. He had meant to make the comment kind of light, but it was difficult for him to keep it light these days.

"I'm sorry," she said.

"Don't apologize," he said. "There's no damned reason to. You didn't do anything. Nobody did."

"I'm not apologizing, not really. I'm just sorry that life is so messed up."

He huffed out a laugh. "You and me both. I'm not sure what you're supposed to do with a bunch of broken pieces," he said, the words torn from him. "When they're all you have left. When you had this full, complete life and then suddenly it's just gone. I don't know what the hell you're supposed to do with that."

"I don't either," she commented. "I really don't.

I guess you try to make a new life, new things. Out of the broken bits."

"I don't think I have the desire or the energy," he said.

"What's the alternative?" she asked, her voice hushed. "I'm not trying to be flippant. I'm asking a serious question. If you don't rebuild, what do you do? Just sit there in the rubble? Because I think you deserve a hell of a lot more than that."

"What's the point? Everything you do, everything you are, can be taken from you." He didn't know what had gotten him into such a dire place. He'd just had sex for the first time in years and now suddenly they were talking about the fragility of life. "All these things you make your identity out of. Husband. Father. Billionaire. They're just things. They get taken from you, and then what? It's like you said about your mother last night. You lose sight of who you are, and then you're just afraid of what will be left. Once you lose those titles that defined you then…then there's just nothing. That's how it feels. Like I'm standing on a hell of a lot of nothing. Somehow I'm not in a free fall…but I don't trust this will last. I don't trust that the whole world won't just fall apart again."

They turned up the dirt road onto her property and didn't speak until they were inside the house again. Then finally she turned to him, her dark eyes full of compassion. He didn't like that. The compassion. Because it was so damned close to pity.

"I don't know what to say," she said, when they got into the house. She looked at him with luminous eyes, and he could read her sincerity. Her sadness.

He didn't want either.

He reached out, grabbing hold of her wrist and wrapping his arm around her waist, crushing her to his body, because he couldn't think of anything else to do. He needed something to hold on to, and she was there, like she had always been. In the middle of that horrible breakdown that he'd had at Eleanor's funeral, she'd been there. And she was here now. There was a yawning, horrific ache inside of him, and she was the only thing he could think of that would fill it.

"I used to be a husband," he said, his voice rough. "I used to be a father. And now I'm just a man with a· hole inside, and I don't know what the hell I'm going to do to fix it. I don't even know if I want to fix it. I don't know who I am."

"I do," she said softly. She lifted the hand that was currently free and brushed her fingertips against the side of his face, tracing the line of his jaw. "You're a man, Knox. A man that I want. For now…can that be enough? Can you just be that for me?"

Everything inside of him roared an enthusiastic hell yes. He could be that. He could do that. It was actually the one damn thing he knew in that moment. That he could be Selena's lover. That he could satisfy them both. He didn't know what the hell was going on in the rest of the world, but he knew what could happen here, in her bedroom.

And so he picked her up, holding her close to his chest as he carried her to the back of the house and deposited her on her bed. He stripped them both of their clothes, leaving the lights on so he could drink his fill of her beautiful body. He was about to do to her what he had done last night, to force her legs open and taste her as deeply as he wanted to. But she sat up on the bed, moving to the edge and pressing her hands to the center of his bare chest.

"Let me," she whispered. She pressed a kiss to his pectoral muscle, right next to his nipple. "Let me show you. Let me show you how much I want you."

He tensed, his entire body drawn tight like a bow. She continued an exploration down his torso, down his stomach, and lower still until she reached his cock. She curved her fingers around him, leaning forward and flicking her tongue over the head. His breath caught sharply, his entire body freezing.

"I've never done this either," she said. He looked down at her and saw that she was making eye contact with him, her expression impish. "If you were wondering."

Of course he had wondered, because he was a man, and damned possessive even if he shouldn't be. And the fact that she was doing this for him, only for him, and had never done it for anyone else was far too pleasing a revelation by half.

She braced herself on his thighs and took him deeper into her mouth, arching her back and sticking her ass in the air. He pressed his palm down between her shoulder blades and tried to keep himself from falling over as she continued to pleasure him with her lips and her tongue. It was a hell of a thing, accepting pleasure like this. He hadn't fully realized what he'd been doing to himself all this time. Punishing himself. Taking everything away that he possibly could.

Sex. Leisure time. All of it.

He hadn't allowed himself to enjoy a damned meal since his daughter's funeral. It was all hurry up and then get back to work. Leave work and then exercise. Work the ranch. It was only during this past week while he'd been here with Selena that he had begun to get in touch with some of the things he had left behind. Things like the company of people he cared about. Like going to an event and seeing people you knew. Like how much he enjoyed the touch of a woman. And he didn't know what he felt about all these revelations—the knowledge that he'd been punishing himself and the fact that he had started letting go of that punishment this week.

Piece by piece.

He felt a sharp pang of guilt join with the overriding sense of pleasure she was pouring onto him with all that sweet, lavish attention from her mouth.

Need was roaring through him now, and it was almost impossible for him to keep himself in check. He knew he needed to, but part of him didn't want to. Part of him just wanted to surrender to this completely, surrender to her completely.

But no, she deserved better than this.

In the end, she deserved better than him, but he was too weak to turn her away.

He didn't have the power. And that was what it always damn well came down to.

That when it came to the important things, he didn't have the strength to make an impact.

But he could make it good for her. And he would take that.

"Not like this," he said, his voice rough.

He grabbed hold of her arms and pulled her up his body, claiming her mouth in a searing kiss, his heart pounding hard, his breath coming in fierce gasps. Then he laid her down on the bed, hooked her leg up over his hip and thrust into her deep and hard, taking her until they were both breathless, until they were both completely caught up and consumed in their release.

When it was over they lay together. Just a man and a woman. Who had wanted each other. Who had needed each other, and who had taken steps to act on that need.

It was simple. Peaceful. He let his mind go blank and just rested. Listened to her breathe in and out. Focused on the feel of her silken skin beneath his touch. The way her hair spread over his chest in a glossy wave.

It didn't last long.

Didn't take long before he remembered who he was. Who they were. Before he had to face the fact that even though he felt like he might have been washed clean by what happened between them, he was still the same. Deep down, he was still the same.

Selena curled more tightly against him and he wrapped his arm around her, relishing the feel of her warmth, of her feminine softness, of her weight against him. Those words, those thoughts, triggered terror inside him. So he pushed it away.

"Are you going to stay away forever again?" she asked, her tone sleepy.

"What do you mean?"

"I mean, this is the first time you've been back to Royal since…well, you know since what. You've been in Wyoming. I had to chase you down over there to even see you."

"I know," he said.

"Is that what we are going to do? Are you going to leave and put distance between yourself and Texas again?"

And between himself and her. That part was unspoken, but he sensed it was there. And that it was a very real concern.

"It's hard to be here," he said. Finally. "The life Cassandra and I made together was here. It was a good life. It's one that I could have lived till the end. This beautiful house… Our beautiful family. It was good. It really was. I made it. I had all the things you think you want when you picture reaching that perfect position in your life. Then it crashed into a wall." He shook his head. "Nobody likes to go back to the scene of an accident. And that's what it feels like to me."

"I can't even imagine," she said, her voice muffled. She buried her face against his bare shoulder and he curled his hand around the back of her head, holding her. It was strange, to touch her like this, so casually. As if it all hadn't changed between them just last night. Because touching her like this felt natural. It felt right.

"Grief is a hell of a thing, though," he said. "It doesn't really matter where you are. It doesn't really care. It's in a smell, a strange moment that for some reason takes you backward in time. It's seeing a little girl that's the same age as Ellie would've been now. Or a little girl the same age she was when she died. Just seeing people walking together. Couples walking through life. It's freezing in the grocery store because you've picked up a box of crackers."

He tried to laugh, but it was hard. "We carry these

crackers in the store. You know, graham crackers. Organic, obviously. And they were her favorite." He cleared his throat but it did nothing to ease the pressure in his chest. "I can't walk by that damn shelf, Selena." The words were broken, tearing through him, leaving him bloody and ragged inside. "Because I remember the way she used to wipe her mouth on my shirt and leave a trail behind. She would just...ruin all these really nice shirts. It was frustrating, and I think it annoyed me, even though I never got mad at her. Because she was just a baby. Just a little girl." It was surreal. Lying there, talking about this. Like he was watching someone else do it. But if it was another man's life, it wouldn't have hurt so much. "I'd give anything—my damned life—to wash graham cracker out of a shirt again."

He felt wetness on his shoulder and he realized she was crying, and then he realized there was an answering wetness on his own cheeks. "I didn't need to stay away from Texas to protect myself. There's no shielding yourself from something like this. I can lose my shit over a fucking cracker."

She buried her face in his chest. "I wish I could fix it," she said. "And those are the most frustrating words I've ever said. Because they don't give you anything. And they don't fix anything."

"Between the two of us I think we have a lot of broken pieces," he said, clearing his throat.

"I guess so."

"I won't stay away this time," he said, moving his hand up and down her bare curves, down her waist, over her hip. "I don't think I could." He was quiet for a long time. "I haven't told anyone that story." She didn't have to ask which one. "I just kept all this stuff to myself."

And he knew it was why his marriage had ended, or at least it was part of the reason why. Because he'd gone inside of himself, and Cassandra had retreated into herself. And neither one of them had known how to find their way back to each other, and they hadn't had the energy—or the desire, really—to even begin to try.

"Thank you for telling me," she said. "Thank you."

"You said you felt like you hadn't done anything. But you have. You did. You gave me this. This memory. This moment. The first thing I've really enjoyed in years. That's not nothing."

"What are friends for?" She smiled, and then she kissed his lips.

And after that, they didn't speak anymore.

Ten

Knox spent the next week at Selena's house, and
he didn't really question what he was doing. Yes,
he had an inkling that he was avoiding his real life.
That he was avoiding dealing with the charity event
that his ex had organized, that he was avoiding the
reality of life in general, but he didn't much want to
focus on any of that.

The mystery surrounding Will's return hadn't
been solved, but there had been no more fake letters and no attempts by anyone to contact Selena.
Knox was leaving all of that to the investigators and
Will's family.

Instead, he wanted to focus on this newfound

layer of his relationship with Selena. Wanted to focus on enjoying the way things felt again. Sex. Food. He and Selena were enjoying a lot of both.

And he was still helping her sort out her property. Slowly, though, because he really wasn't in a hurry to finish. He was working out in the shed, while Selena took care of some business things in the house, when his phone rang.

It was from a number he didn't recognize, so he picked it up just in case it was a business call. "Hello?"

"Knox," the voice on the other end said.

Cassandra. The impact hit him like a punch to the stomach. And his initial response was rage. Absolute rage that she was intruding on this peaceful moment in his life. On this new thing that was happening with him.

He didn't want to hear her voice. Not while he was standing here in Selena's shed, mounting a new shelf so she had adequate storage.

"I don't know this number," he said.

"I got a new phone," she responded, her voice tenuous.

"Why did you call?"

And he felt like an ass for being impatient with her. For being such a jerk, because it wasn't like she had ever done anything to him. They had never really done anything to each other, and that had been the problem in the end.

"You never responded to the invitation for the Ellie's House fundraiser," she said.

"Did I need to? I wrote a check."

"I want you there," she said. "Ellie's House is really important to me. It's the only thing that makes me feel like what I went through—what we went through—wasn't completely pointless and cruel. I want this to be important to you. I want you to be there. To lend your connections. Your appearance matters."

"Don't say it like that," he said. "Don't say it like the charity isn't important to me. Like *she's* not important to me."

There was a long pause on the other end. "I didn't mean it like that. I really didn't. I did not call to have a fight with you, I swear."

He shifted, looking out the door of the shed at the field and trees off in the distance. The leaves blowing in the breeze, the sun shining down on it all. Like the world wasn't really a dark and terrible place. Like he wasn't being torn to shreds every time he took a breath. "We didn't fight while we were married. What's the point in fighting now?"

That produced another long silence. "There isn't one." Cassandra took a breath. "It would mean a lot to me if you could come. And I need to tell you something. Something that…I don't know how to say. I don't know…where to begin."

His chest tightened. "What?"

"Knox... I...I'm getting married."

He had not expected that. Neither had he expected the accompanying feeling of being slapped across the face with a two-by-four. "What?"

"I met someone." Something in her voice changed. Softened. Warmed. Happiness, he realized. He hadn't heard it in her voice in a long time. Certainly not when talking to him. "I didn't expect it. I wasn't looking for it. I didn't even want it. But he's... He makes me happy. And I didn't think I could be happy again. I have purpose with Ellie's House, and...I really want you to come. And I want you to see him. To meet him."

"I'm sorry—why the hell would I want to meet your fiancé, Cassandra?" he asked. He could feel his old life slipping away. Moving into the distance.

Or maybe she was moving on and life was going past him.

"You don't love me," she said. "You're not *in* love with me, anyway."

That wasn't even close to being part of the visceral, negative reaction to her announcement. That much he knew. He didn't want Cassandra. He'd had her, they'd had each other, and they hadn't tried to fix things.

There was something else. Something he couldn't pinpoint. But it wasn't about wanting her back.

"No," he said.

"But we still care about each other, don't we? We were together for ten years. It's such a long time. Our whole twenties. It was you and me. We went through something… You're the only other person on earth who will ever know how I feel. You're the only person who experienced the same losses as me. You'll always matter to me for that reason. I just need you there. I need this closure. Please come."

Those words hit him hard. And somehow, he found that he didn't have the strength to turn her down. "Okay."

"Bring somebody," she said. "I mean it. Find a date. Find…something. We deserve to be happy."

After that, they got off the phone, and he struggled with his feelings about what she'd said. Because at the end of the day, he wasn't entirely sure he deserved to be happy.

He stumbled out of the shed and went into the house. Selena was sitting in there, her dark hair piled up on top of her head in a messy bun. She was holding a pen in her mouth and staring down at her laptop.

She was so damned beautiful he could barely breathe. "Hey," he said.

She looked up and she smiled at him, and it felt like the sun coming out from behind the clouds. Which, for a man who had spent the past two years in darkness, was a pretty big thing.

"Do you want to come to a charity thing with me?"

"Sure," she said, giving him a strange look.

"It's Cassandra's thing," he said.

"Oh," Selena said, her expression cautious. "For Ellie's House?"

He frowned. "You know about that?"

She bit her lip. "About the foundation, yes. I wasn't invited to any charity event. But I sent some money in a while back."

He cleared his throat and shoved his hands into his pockets. "Well, she told me to bring a date."

The corners of her lips turned upward, just slightly. "Then I'm happy to fulfill that role."

"Great," he said, trying to force a smile.

It was only later that he questioned the decision. He realized he was committing to bringing Selena to a public function, as his date. Which had less to do with how it might look—he didn't care, and anyway, it was well established that they were friends—but that he was bringing her along as a plus-one to his grief. That he was basically submitting himself to showing it all to the public.

But it was too late now. He'd already agreed. He'd already asked her to come with him. He was just going to have to get a handle on himself. To get some of his control back.

Because everything was moving in a direction he wasn't sure he liked. All that was left to do was try and keep a handle on himself.

* * *

Knox acted strange for the next week. Which was not helped at all by the fact that Selena was starting to feel a little bit strange herself.

She was trying not to dwell on it. Was trying not to dwell on anything other than the good feelings Knox created in her. Who knew how long all this would last? She didn't want to waste any time being upset or worried. Didn't want to waste time being hypersensitive to his moods or to her own.

There was way too much good happening. And she knew it was temporary. So she planned to just pull herself together and enjoy.

She tried to shake off her lethargy as she looked in the mirror and finished putting her makeup on. She was just so tired. She didn't know if it was because of the lack of sleep since Knox had moved in, or what. Stress, maybe, from the upcoming event for Ellie's House.

Because as much as she knew that he wasn't making a statement by bringing her, it still felt momentous that he'd asked her to come with him. He would probably be annoyed with her for thinking that. But she was coming to an event with his ex-wife and his ex-wife's fiancé. An event for a charity his ex-wife had created for the daughter they had lost.

He could have easily gone by himself. And Selena had a feeling that a few months ago that was exactly what he would have opted to do. Since he had been doing things on his own for the past couple of years.

The fact that he'd reached out to her was probably why he was acting weird. The intensity of the whole situation. She really couldn't blame him.

She checked her reflection in the mirror and had a momentary feeling of uncertainty. And then a flash of jealousy followed closely by a bite of guilt.

She had to wonder if he might compare her to his tall, blonde ex, who was more willowy than she was curvy. And Selena wouldn't really be able to blame him if he did. She and Cassandra were so different. The idea of standing next to Cassandra and playing a game of compare and contrast had been making her feel ill.

Of course, that wasn't what was going to happen. And Cassandra had always been very nice to her.

It'd been strange when she and Knox had gotten divorced, because Selena had genuinely liked her. As much as you could like the woman who had ended up with the man of your dreams, *obviously*.

But as Selena had recused herself from having those kinds of dreams, she'd never really been angry with Cassandra. Knox being married had always been both a relief and a heartache. There was really no other way to describe it. A relief because that feeling of *what if* had abated slightly since there had been no more *what if* left. But also it had just burned sometimes. Knowing he was with someone else. That he'd loved someone else.

But she'd never let herself dwell on it. She hadn't been able to be with him romantically, not when a relationship like that would have required risk and a trust she hadn't been willing to give. But she'd also needed him in her life, and she wasn't about to let something like a marriage come between them.

Now, had Cassandra been a bad wife, Selena wouldn't have been able to stand for it. But Cassandra had always been great. Exactly the kind of woman Selena thought Knox should have been with. So getting all bent out of shape about Cassandra and comparisons now was just pointless.

She twisted her body slightly, frowning as she smoothed her hand over the front of her fitted gold dress. A strange sense of disquiet raced through her as she adjusted herself in the halter top. Her breasts hurt. Like they were bruised.

That was very, very strange.

She knew of only one thing that caused such intense breast tenderness and…no. That was ridiculous. Except her breasts had never been tender before. Her eyes dropped down to her stomach. She looked the same. She couldn't believe…couldn't believe there could be a baby in there.

And the first time…she and Knox had forgotten condoms. That had been in the back of her mind, niggling at her consciousness, ever since. At the time, it had been lost in confessions of her virginity and the deep pain he'd expressed when talking about his daughter.

But the fact remained…the condoms had been forgotten.

The stomach she was currently scrutinizing felt as though it dropped down to her toes.

She could not be pregnant. Well, she could be pregnant—that was the trouble. She really could be. She and Knox had unprotected sex and she was… Well, she was late.

"No," she said to her reflection, bracing her arms on the dresser. "No," she said.

"What's going on?"

She turned around to see Knox standing there wearing a suit and a black tie, and if her stomach hadn't already been down in her toes, it would have done a full free fall.

"Nothing," she said, turning around quickly, still holding on to the dresser. "I just was afraid that I couldn't find my earrings. But I did."

"The ones you're wearing?"

"No," she said, grabbing for another pair on top of the cluttered dresser. "These."

And he kept staring at her, so she had to change into the earrings that she had already decided against. She took out the pair that looked absolutely perfect with her gold dress and sadly discarded them on the top of the dresser. Then she put the others in, smiling. "See?"

"Right," he said, clearly not seeing a distinction between the two. Because he was a man. Which was the only reason that her excuse actually worked. Because otherwise he would know that the other pair was clearly better.

"Are you ready to go?"

"Yes," she said.

"I got us a room at the hotel where the charity event is being held. You know, so that neither of us has to be the designated driver."

He was keeping his tone light, but she definitely sensed the hint of strain beneath it.

"Sounds good," she said.

At the mention of alcohol, she realized that she actually couldn't bring herself to drink a glass of champagne before she knew for sure.

Before she knew for sure if she was pregnant.

Oh, she was going to pass out. She really was. She wasn't sure how she was supposed to get through tonight. She needed to sneak away from him and get a test.

This wasn't happening.

It wasn't fair.

It definitely couldn't crash into the event tonight, because the event was way too important. For the memory of his daughter.

Suddenly, Selena was sure she was going to throw up.

"Are you okay?"

"I guess," she said. "I'm nervous." She opted to be honest about part of her problem so she could leave out the big, scary part. "I haven't seen Cassandra since your divorce. And the two of us are... You know."

"She's engaged," he said.

"It's not her that I'm worried about."

He frowned. "Are you afraid I'm going to see her and want her? Instead of you?"

"I don't know," she said, lifting a shoulder. "Yes."

"I'm not harboring secret feelings for Cassandra," he said. "We'll always be... We're linked. She and I created a life together. And then we both had to go through the experience of losing it. Losing Ellie. So it's not the same as if we were sharing custody or something. But..."

"I'm all right with that. I mean, I get it. I really do. And I am not upset about that at all. I just... She's prettier than me," Selena said finally.

He frowned. "You are the prettiest damned woman, Selena Jacobs," he said. He reached out and brushed his fingertips across her cheek. "I...I haven't felt this good in a long time. And the fact that I still feel pretty good even with all of this Ellie's House stuff looming on the horizon... It's a testament to you. I don't long for my marriage. The man who was married to Cassandra doesn't exist anymore. That's the only real way I can think to explain it. We changed too much and we didn't change together. Nobody's fault. It just is. But the woman she is now has found a different man. The man I am now wants you. Nobody else. I can't even compare the two of you. I don't want to. You're you. You always have been. You occupy a special place in my life no one else ever has."

Her heart felt swollen, like it might burst through her chest. It wasn't quite a declaration of love, but it almost was. He put his arm around her and started to guide her out of the bedroom, and then they headed to the driveway, where he got into the driver's side of her car and started down the road that would take them to downtown Royal for the event.

This felt right, being with him for this event to celebrate his daughter's memory. She had to wonder what that meant. She had been so convinced that there was no future between herself and him. Had been utterly and completely certain that the two of them could have nothing but sex and friendship.

But they were in some different space where all those pieces had woven together, and her feelings for him were so big. So deep and real. She just didn't know where they were anymore. And she wondered why she was resisting at all. Because when she had decided she wasn't going to have a husband and children, when she had decided that love wasn't for her, that idea had been attached to an abstract man. Some version of her father who might someday betray her.

But this relationship she'd started wasn't with an abstract man. It certainly wasn't with anyone who resembled her father.

It was with *Knox*.

Knox, who had been one of her best friends for all of her adult life. She trusted him, more than she trusted just about anybody. She wasn't afraid of him. She wasn't afraid of loving him. He was a safe place for all those feelings to land.

And if she was having his baby…

She had no idea what to make of that. Had no idea what it would mean to him. She knew he'd said he didn't want to have a relationship again, but what if they were having a child? What would that do to him?

Suddenly, the whole situation seemed a lot more fraught than it had a moment ago. Just one moment of peace, and then it had evaporated.

Surely he would want another child, though—if she was really pregnant. He had been a wonderful father, and it wasn't as if a new baby would replace the little girl he had lost.

Her brain was still tying itself in knots when they arrived at the hotel. Cars and limousines were circling the area in front, valets taking the vehicles away to be parked, doormen ushering people inside. Knox stuck his black cowboy hat on his head and smiled at her, and then the two of them got out of the car and headed into the hotel. She clung to him, mostly because she thought if she let go of him she might collapse completely.

And not just because of those strange feelings of jealousy she'd had earlier. No, not at all. It had very little to do with that. It was just...everything else. Suddenly, what she and Knox were doing, what they were sharing, felt too big.

They made their way into the lobby of the hotel. It was art deco with inlaid geometric designs on the floor reflected in gold on the ceiling panels. There was a banner hung over the main ballroom, welcoming the distinguished attendees to the first annual fundraiser for Ellie's House.

But it was the picture on the stand, right in the entry of the ballroom, that stopped her short and made her breath freeze in her chest. It was a photograph of a little girl. Beautiful. Blonde.

With the same gray eyes as her daddy.

She was lying in a field with her hands propped beneath her chin, yellow-and-purple wildflowers blooming all around her.

Selena's heart squeezed tight and she fought to take a breath. She clung even more tightly to Knox, whose posture was rigid. She sneaked a glance at him and saw that he was holding his jaw almost impossibly tense. It hurt her to see that picture. In memoriam of a child who would be here if life was fair. She couldn't imagine how it was for him.

He paused for just a moment, and she looked away as he brushed his fingertips lightly over the portrait. It felt wrong to watch that. Like she was intruding on a private moment. On a greeting or a goodbye. She wasn't sure.

He straightened, then began moving forward. She rested her head on his shoulder as they walked, and she had a feeling they were holding each other up now.

The ornate room was filling up, but it didn't take long for her to spot Cassandra, her blond hair pulled back into a bun. She was all pointed shoulders and collarbones, much thinner than she had been the last time Selena had seen her. But as beautiful as ever. Cassandra had always been a stunning woman, and tonight was no exception. She was wearing an understated black dress, with a ribbon pinned to the top.

She rushed over to greet them, her expression harried, her face a bit pale. "I'm so glad you made it," she said. She took a step forward, like she was ready to hug Knox, and then thought better of it. Instead, she reached into her clutch and produced two ribbons, pressing them into Knox's palm. "If you want to wear these."

"Thank you," he said.

"Hi," Cassandra said to Selena.

Selena broke the awkwardness and leaned in, embracing Cassandra in a hug. "Hi," she said. "It's good to see you."

Cassandra looked between them, her expression full of speculation, but she said nothing. Instead, she just twisted the large yellow diamond ring on her left hand.

"Is your fiancé here?" Knox asked.

"He was," Cassandra said. "I sent him out to get me some new nylons because I put a run in mine. He's good like that."

"He sounds it," he said, a slight smile curving his lips.

"Well," Cassandra said. "You know me. If there is a nylon in the vicinity I will cause a run in it."

"I'm glad you have someone to get you a new pair," he said.

"Me, too." After a beat of silence, she said, "I'm sorry—I have to go back to getting everything in order, but I'll find you again later tonight."

"You're gonna make tons of money," he said.

"I hope so," she said. "I hope we do. I hope I am part of making sure that in the future this doesn't happen. Not to anyone." Cassandra's blue eyes filled with tears and she looked away. When she looked back at Knox, her smile was in place. "Sorry. I have to go."

She turned abruptly, brushing her hands over her face, her slim shoulders rising and falling on a long breath. Then she strode forward resolutely, mingling with the other people who were starting to fill up the ballroom.

Selena could only be impressed with the way that Knox handled himself the whole evening. He had pinned the ribbon that Cassandra had given him proudly on his lapel, and Selena had done the same, to the top of her dress. And she did her very best to keep her focus on what was happening around them. Ellie's House—Ellie's memory—was simply too important for Selena to get caught up in her own worries.

There was a buffet, which Selena noticed Knox never went near. And she made a point of acting like she hadn't noticed. But when the band started to play, she asked him to dance.

He surprised her by complying.

He swept her into his arms, and for the first time in hours, she felt like things might be okay between them. "This is a wonderful tribute," she said, softly.

"Yes," he responded, the word clipped.

"I'm sorry." She lowered her head. "I said the wrong thing."

"No. It's just…still hard to accept that my daughter needs tributes. I guess I should be more used to it by now."

"No. Don't do that, Knox. You were caught off guard earlier."

"It was a nice picture," he said, his voice rough.

"I remember the day it was taken. Out at the Jackson Hole ranch where we used to take picnics. I don't…I don't even like to remember. Even the good times hurt."

Selena didn't say anything. She just rested her head against his chest and swayed with him on the dance floor. They didn't speak much for the rest of the evening. Knox focused on talking to potential donors, rather than to her. But Selena was used to these types of events and it was easy for her to go off and do the same, to make sure she did her part to bring in money for the charity.

Cassandra gave an amazing speech about the importance of medical research, and the progress that was being made in the effort to treat childhood cancers and other childhood diseases. She talked about the function of the charity, how they donated money to innovative research teams and to housing for the various hospitals, so families could stay near their children while they received treatment and not be buried under the financial burden.

Selena found that she could only be impressed with Knox's ex-wife. She couldn't be jealous. She was just proud. And it seemed…okay then, that Knox would always have a connection with Cassandra. It seemed important even. Selena certainly wanted to be involved in supporting this effort with Ellie's House, and she thought it was amazing what Cassandra had done with her grief.

As the clock drew closer to midnight, Selena hit a wall, so tired that she was barely able to stand. Knox, on the other hand, was still moving dynamically around the room, stumping to have more checks written. It was amazing to watch the way the fire had been lit inside of him since they had arrived. Clearly he had a desire to make all of his family's suffering count for something. To make the loss count for something.

Suddenly she felt so nauseous, she thought she might collapse. Fuzzy-headed. Sleepy. It could just be stress and fatigue. It had been a crazy few weeks and a hard evening. She was just so overly…done.

She walked over to Knox and touched his arm. "I need to go to bed," she said.

He gave her a cursory glance, obviously still focused on the event. Which was fine with her. She imagined he would want to stay till the end. She *wanted* to stay; she was just going to fall over if she tried.

"I'll see you up in the room," he responded.

If he was disappointed about the fact that she would be asleep when he got there, rather than ready for sex, he didn't show it. But then, he was busy. And she could appreciate that. She could more than appreciate that. It was good to see him passionate about something, especially something involving his daughter's memory. Good to see him involved.

Selena slipped out the back of the ballroom and

wrapped her arms around her midsection as she walked through the lobby. She felt so awful. So tired she thought she might fall asleep where she stood.

And though it *could* be stress and fatigue.

Or something a lot scarier.

There was only one way to find out whether or not she was carrying Knox's baby.

Maybe the timing sucked, and she should just go to bed. But now that she started thinking about the possibility again, she couldn't wait. Not another minute, and certainly not until tomorrow morning.

She stopped walking, pausing for a moment in front of the concierge desk. Then she took a tentative step forward.

"Is there a pharmacy close by?"

Eleven

Knox felt guilty about letting Selena leave the party without him. But he was engaged in a pretty intense conversation with a local business mogul about donations and ways to raise awareness, and he felt… like he was able to do something. Like he could be something other than helpless.

Tonight, Cassandra made much more sense to him. She had thrown herself into this. At first, her drive had been difficult for him. Because every reminder of Eleanor was a painful one. But now, after participating in the fundraiser, he understood.

Looking around at all of this, he couldn't help but understand. She was doing the only thing she could. Her mother's heart compelled her to let their daughter live on somehow, while Knox had been consumed in the grief.

He hadn't had it in him to take that kind of generous approach. To make sure what had happened to his daughter didn't happen to anyone else. But he had found it tonight. He had found something that he had thought long gone—hope. Like there was a future in this world that was worth being part of.

And that made him feel...like a little piece of himself had been recovered. A piece he had thought he might never access again. A piece that allowed him to be a part of the world, that allowed him to enjoy being alive. To enjoy the taste of food. The touch of a woman. The desire to accomplish something. Anything.

And, yes, the fundraiser had made a difference, but the catalyst for this change was all Selena.

As the night wore on, the crowds began to thin out, and finally, he was left with Cassandra, who sat up on the stage. She looked exhausted, and she looked sad.

"You did a good thing," he said, walking over and taking a spot next to her.

"Thank you," she said, treating him to a tired smile. "But I know."

"Isn't this exhausting?" he asked.

"What?" she asked. "Charity events?"

"Reliving this all the time," he said.

"I do anyway," she said. "So why not make something of it? This charity helps me feel like I'm moving on. Even though it all…stems from her, losing her. I don't know how to explain it, really. Like I'm taking the tragedy and making something positive with it."

He looked across the room and saw Cassandra's fiancé, who was helping with cleanup. He seemed like a good man. A great man. One who had jumped into all of this without having known Ellie at all, but who supported the charity just because it meant so much to Cassandra.

It occurred to Knox then that the truth of the matter was that Cassandra *was* a hell of a lot more moved on than he was.

And he didn't know what to feel about that. He didn't know how to reconcile it. He didn't know if he *wanted* to move on.

And yet moving on was what he had just been thinking about. That experience of beginning to enjoy life again.

Was that what she had now? Could she be thankful to be alive? Was she able to love this man? And not be afraid of loss?

Part of him still wanted to hold on to the past. Wanted to fight against blurry images, fading pain and the normalcy he was starting to feel on some days. Wanted to fight against the past slipping away. He wanted to go back out front and stare at that portrait of his daughter lying in a field of flowers. To memorize her face.

He just didn't want to forget.

He didn't *want* to come out the other side of this grief.

Suddenly, he felt like he was sliding down into a dark pit, and he had no idea what in hell to do about it. If he wanted to do anything about it at all. He had no idea what to do with any of these feelings. Had no idea what had happened to the good feelings from a few moments before, and even less of an idea about why he resented having those good feelings now.

Grief didn't make sense. All of the guides talked about stages and moving on. For him, it wasn't stages. It was waves, coming and going, drowning him. The memory of his child acting like a life raft in his mind.

How the hell could he move on from his own life raft?

Cassandra had said earlier that he was the only person who had been through what she had been through. And that was true. But now he was sitting here alone with these feelings. She had moved on. And there was no one. No one at all.

It scared him.

What would happen if they both went on with their lives like Ellie hadn't existed? If she became only this monument to a greater cause, instead of the child they loved so much.

And suddenly, he needed to get out of there. Suddenly, he needed to find Selena.

He knew she was asleep, but he needed her.

"I'm going up to bed," he said, and if his departure seemed sudden, he didn't much care. He walked out of the ballroom and headed through the lobby, getting into the elevator and checking the key in his wallet to see which room he and Selena were in. Then he pushed the appropriate button and headed up to their floor.

He got to the room and pushed the key card into the door, opening it slowly. When he got inside, Selena was not asleep as he'd expected.

She was sitting on the edge of the bed, her head bent down. She looked up, her face streaked with makeup and tears and a horrific sense of regret.

"What's going on?" he asked. "I thought you were going to sleep."

Then he looked down at her hands. At the white stick she was clutching between her fingers.

The look on Knox's face mirrored what she was feeling.

Terror. Sheer, unmitigated terror.

But even through the terror, she knew they could do this. They would get through it as they had every other thing life had thrown at them over the years. They would make it work together.

She trusted him, and that was the mantra she kept repeating to herself, over and over again.

She had given Knox her heart slowly over the past decade. And now he had all of it, along with her trust.

She loved him.

She always had. But sitting there looking at the test results, she knew she was in love with him. The kind of love built to withstand. The kind that could endure.

She loved him.

They could weather this. She was confident they could.

"I'm sorry," she said. "I didn't want you to find out like this."

She had fully intended to talk to him tomorrow, but then she had ended up sitting on the edge of the bed, unable to move. Completely and utterly shell-shocked by what was in front of her in pink and white.

The incontrovertible truth that she was pregnant with Knox McCoy's baby.

She had cried, but she wasn't sad. Not really. It was just so much to take in, especially after spending the evening at the charity event. Especially after seeing the portrait of his daughter by the door and witnessing all the small ways grief affected him. The small ways that loss took chunks out of him over the course of an evening like this.

Now he was finding out about this. It just seemed a bit much.

"You're pregnant," he said.

"Yes. We didn't… We forgot a couple of times," she said, her voice muted.

That first time, down at the camp.

That second night, in her room when they had talked about Eleanor and graham crackers and her heart had broken for him in ways she hadn't thought she could recover from.

"I can't do this," he said, his voice rough.

"I mean…" She tried to swallow but it was like her throat was lined with the inside of a pincushion. "A baby isn't tea. I can't…not serve it to you. I can't… Maybe this is our sign we have to try something real, Knox."

The words came out weak and she despised herself for them.

"I can't," he said again.

Her heart thundered so hard it hurt. Felt sharp. Like it was cutting its way out of her chest.

"We *can*," she said. "We can do this together, Knox. I know that it's not…ideal."

"Not ideal?" he asked, his words fraying around the edges. "*Not ideal* is a damned parking ticket, Selena. This is not *acceptable*."

Anger washed through her, quick and sharp. At him. At herself. At how unfair the whole world was. They should just be able to have this. To be happy.

But they couldn't because life was hard, and it had stolen so much from him. She hurt for him; she did.

But oh, right now she hurt so much for herself.

"I'm sorry that the pregnancy is unacceptable to you, but it's too late. I'm pregnant."

"Selena…"

"I love you," she said. "I didn't want to say that right now either. I didn't want to do it like this, but… Knox, I love you. And I know that I've always said I didn't want a husband and children, but I could do it with you. If we are going to have a baby then I can do it. I *want* to do it."

She straightened her shoulders as she said the words, realizing just then that she was committing to her baby. "I…I want this baby."

He looked at her for a moment, his eyes unreadable.

"Then you're going to have it on your own."

She felt like she had been blasted through with a cannonball, that it had left her completely hollowed out. Nothing at all remaining.

Pain radiated from her chest, outward. Climbing up her throat and making it feel so tight she couldn't breathe.

"You don't want this?"

"I can't."

She felt for him. For his loss. She truly did. But it wasn't just her being wounded. It was their child.

A child who was losing a chance at having him for a father.

She had thought…

She had no idea how she could have misjudged this—misjudged him—so completely.

She'd thought…if she knew one person on earth well enough to trust them it should have been him.

This was her nightmare.

But it wasn't just heartbreak over losing the man she loved, over losing the future she'd so briefly imagined for them before he walked into their suite.

No, she was losing her friend.

And bringing a child into the heartache.

"So that's it. You don't want to be a father again." Dread, loss, sadness…it all poured through her in a wave. She felt like she was back in the river with him, but this time, he was pushing her under instead of holding her up. "You don't want me."

"Selena, I already told you. I've had this. I've had it, and I lost it, and I cannot do this again. There is no mystery left in the damned world for me. I know what it's like to bury my child, Selena. I will not… I can never love another child like that. Ever."

She had trusted him.

That was all she could think as she stood there, getting ripped to shreds by his words.

As a young woman, she had been convinced that the hardest thing, the most difficult thing in the world, was enduring being beaten by a man with his fists. Her father had kicked her, punched her while she was down.

But this hurt so much worse. This was a loss so deep she could scarcely fathom it. This was pain, real and unending.

She couldn't process it.

She pressed her hand against her stomach. "Then go," she said, her mouth numb, her tongue thick. "Go. Because I'm not going to expose my child to your indifference. I'm not going to be my mother, Knox. I'm not going to have a man in my child's life who doesn't care about them."

"Selena."

"No. You're the one who said it. Why couldn't my mother love me enough to make sure I was in the best situation possible? Why didn't she protect me? Well, now I'm the mother, the one making choices. I'm going to love this baby enough for both of us. I'm going to give it everything I never had and everything you refuse to give it. Now get the hell away from me."

He was operating from a place of grief, and she knew it, but he was an adult. She knew full well that her duty was to protect her child, not Knox's emotional state.

She was sick, and she was angry. And she didn't think she would ever recover.

"I just can't," he reiterated, moving toward the door of the hotel room.

"Then don't," she said. "But I don't believe the man who pulled himself up out of poverty, got himself into Harvard, stood by me as a good friend for all those years and came to Will's funeral, even though it was hard—I don't believe that man can't do this. What I believe is that you're very good at shutting people out. You go into yourself when it gets hard, rather than reaching out. Reach out to me, Knox. Let's do this together. I don't need it to be perfect or easy. We have a bunch of broken pieces between us, but let's try to make something new with them."

"I can't." He looked at her one more time with horribly flat, dark eyes, and then he turned and walked out of the hotel room, leaving her standing in a shimmering gold ball gown, ready to dissolve into a puddle of misery on the floor.

There was pain, and then there was this.

Knowing she was having her best friend's baby. And that she would be raising that baby alone.

Twelve

He drank all the way back to Jackson Hole. He drank more in the back of the car as his driver took him back to the ranch. And he kept on drinking all the way until he got back to his house and passed out in bed. When he woke up, he had no idea what time it was, but the sun was shining through the window and his head was pounding like a son of a bitch. He was also still a little bit drunk.

Best of both worlds.

He could hardly believe what had happened earlier. It all seemed like a dream. Like maybe he had never gone to Royal and had never gone to a funeral for Will that hadn't actually happened. Like maybe he had never slept with Selena. He had never gone to that charity event in honor of his daughter. And then Selena certainly hadn't told him she was pregnant with his baby.

Because why the hell would she be pregnant with his baby since certainly they had never really slept together?

And they certainly hadn't been living together like a couple. Playing house, reenacting the life that he had lost. A life he could never have again.

He got up and saw half a tumbler full of scotch sitting on the nightstand. He drained it quickly, relishing the burn as he fumbled for his phone. He checked to see if he had any missed calls and saw that he didn't. But he did see that it was about three in the afternoon.

He frowned down at his phone for a long moment, then scrolled through his contacts. "Hello?"

"Cassandra," he said, the words slurred.

"Knox?"

"Yes," he said. "I am drunk."

"I can tell." She paused, because clearly she wasn't going to help him with this conversation. She wasn't going to tell him why he had called. He wished she would. He sure as hell didn't have a clue. Didn't know why he was reaching out to her now when he hadn't done it during their marriage.

When he hadn't been able to do it when it might have fixed something.

"Are you all right?" she pressed.

"Fuck no," he said. "I am not all right."

"Okay." Again, she gave him nothing.

"How come you're happy?" he asked. "I'm not happy. I don't want to be happy. What happens if both of us are happy and we forget about her? We forget how much it hurt? And how much she mattered?"

He heard her stifle a sob on the other end of the line. "We won't. We won't."

"What if we do?" His heart felt like it was cracking in two. "I don't want to replace her. I can't."

"You won't," she said. "You won't replace her ever. Why would you think that?"

"Selena is pregnant," he said, "and I don't know what to do. Because it's like I traded our life in for a new version. That's not fair to anyone. It's just not."

His words didn't make any sense, but all he knew was that everything hurt, and he couldn't make sense of any of it.

There were no words for this particular deep well of pain inside of him.

"You're not," she said, her voice cracking. "You're *not*."

"I'm sorry," he said. "I think I called to be mad at you. For being okay. For moving on. But now I'm just sorry. I should've been there for you. Maybe we should have been there better for each other."

"Maybe," she said. "But I didn't want to be."

Silence fell between them. "I didn't either."

"I loved our life," she said. "And it took me a long time to realize that I think I loved our life more than we loved each other. And when we lost Ellie… It wasn't that life anymore. And what we'd had wasn't enough to hold us together."

"Yeah," he agreed, her words making a strange kind of sense in his alcohol-soaked brain. "Yeah, I think so."

"You need to find somebody you love no matter the circumstances. Not just someone you love because she fits a piece in your life. Because she fulfills a role. Not a wife—a partner."

"I'm afraid," he said, the words ripped from somewhere down deep.

Cassandra laughed, soft and sympathetic. "Join the club. Believe me. Nobody is more afraid than me. I mean, maybe you. But it's hard. It's hard to open yourself up again. I think so… I think you already did. I think you're already in love. So don't keep yourself from it. That's not protecting yourself. That's just punishing yourself. And if that's what you're really doing…you need to stop."

"How?" he asked. "How am I supposed to stop punishing myself when I'm here and she's gone? When I couldn't protect her? How am I supposed to move on from that?"

When Cassandra spoke again, her voice was small. "You have to move on from it, Knox, because she isn't here anymore. And as little as either of us could do for her when she was ill, there's nothing we can do for her now. There's nothing you can do by holding on to your grief. She doesn't need you anymore. She doesn't need this from you."

He couldn't speak. His throat was too tight, his chest was too tight and everything hurt.

"Selena *needs* you," Cassandra continued. "The child you're going to have with her needs you. And you're going to have to figure out a way to be there for her, for this child, or you really aren't the man I met all those years ago."

He couldn't speak after that. And Cassandra let him off the hook, saying goodbye and hanging up the phone.

Because he wasn't that man. He wasn't. He didn't know how to be. He didn't want to be. He was changed. Hollowed out and scarred. Like a forest that had been ravaged by wildfire, leaving behind nothing but dead, charred wood.

Selena needed him.

Cassandra's words continued to echo through him. Selena needed him. Not Eleanor. Eleanor was gone, and it was unfair. But there was nothing he could do about it but grieve. And he knew he would do that for all of his life. There was no way to let go of something like that. Not truly. But maybe there was a way to learn to live. To live with the grief inside of you, to allow good memories to come back in and take residence alongside the pain.

To let love be there next to it, too.

Maybe moving on wasn't about being the man he used to be. Maybe it was about doing what Selena had said. Maybe it was about making something new out of the broken pieces.

Selena needed him. Their baby needed him.

He was beginning to suspect he needed Selena, too. That without her he was going to sink into the darkness forever.

The question was whether or not he wanted to let in the light.

Selena had gone to the doctor to confirm her pregnancy after securing someone else's canceled appointment, and then had gone to Paradise Farms to visit Scarlett and see how baby Carl was doing. While she watched her bright-eyed friend play with her new baby, Selena felt a strange mix of pain and hope.

She had made choices to protect her baby. To protect this little life growing inside of her that she already loved so much.

Watching Scarlett brought it all into full Technicolor. Made impending motherhood feel real.

"Do you like it?"

"What?" Scarlett asked, looking up from Carl's play.

"Being a mother."

"That's a funny question."

Selena lifted a shoulder. "I'm in a funny mood. Indulge me."

"Yes. Although there are periods where I'm so tired I just want to lie on the floor and sleep." She shifted her hold on the baby and looked down at him, smiling. "And I have done that. Believe me. Sometimes I ask myself why I made this choice. Why I decided to have a baby before I had a life. But…I do like it. Adopting Carl has been the most rewarding thing I've ever done. Even though sometimes it's really hard. But I love him. And adding love to your life is never a bad thing."

Selena tapped the side of her mug of tea, looking out the window. "I like that. It's adding love."

"And a lot of work," Scarlett said. "Are you thinking about adopting?"

Her friend was likely joking, judging by the lightness in her tone. Because Selena had never given any indication she had an interest in adopting a baby. In fact, she was probably the least maternal person Scarlett knew. There was no way to ease her friend into this. No way to broach the subject gently.

So Selena figured it was time to drop the bombshell. "No, I'm not thinking of adopting. I'm pregnant."

Scarlett stared at Selena in shocked silence, opening and closing her mouth like a fish that had been chucked onto dry land. When she finally recovered her ability to speak, it came out as a shocked squeak. *"What?"*

Selena looked down into her teacup. Tea leaves were supposed to tell the future. Her Yorkshire Gold only contained the reflection of her own downtrodden expression. "It happened on the camping trip."

"Damn," Scarlett said. "I guess those tents really are romantic."

"Romance wasn't required," Selena said, grimacing. "It was more than a decade of pent-up lust."

She sighed and leaned back on the couch. "But he's not ready for this. He doesn't want anything to do with me."

Scarlett frowned. "He doesn't? That's just… I don't know him that well, but everything I do know about him suggests that he's a better man than that."

"He is," Selena said. "He's a good man. But he's also a scared man. He's not doing a very good job of handling his fear. It just got all messed up. I found out I was pregnant the night we were at the gala fundraiser for the charity his ex-wife created in honor of their daughter. He freaked out. And I kind of don't blame him. The night was an emotional marathon."

Her eyes filled with tears, and her throat felt strange, like she had swallowed a sword, making it painful to breathe. "I only just found out I was pregnant and I got it confirmed today. And while I was sitting there waiting for the lab results to come in I just… It already hurt to think that I might lose the baby. That maybe I wasn't really pregnant or something had gone wrong with the first test. I don't even have a little person to hold in my arms yet and my love is so big. Knox lost a child... I'm angry at him for hurting me. But I can't fathom what he's gone through, the grief he feels. And as much as he deserves it, I can't even hate him for walking away."

"You don't need to hate him," Scarlett said. "You might need to punch him in the junk."

"I don't want to do that either. Okay. I want to do it a little bit. But I just... I'll do this parenthood thing by myself. You're doing it, right? I'll raise the baby. I can take care of us. I have plenty of money. My child is never going to want for anything."

Scarlett looked down at Carl and stroked a finger over his downy cheek. "You're going to be a good mother."

"You say that with a lot of confidence."

"Because I know you. You'll probably be tired, and you'll probably make mistakes. I know I'm making mistakes all the time. But it all comes back to the love. Love covers a whole lot of things, Selena. I truly believe that."

"I just wish love could cover this." Tears she hadn't even been aware of began to slide down her cheeks. "I love Knox so much. I want him. For me. For the baby. But I also just wish he could have had a different life. Even if it meant losing him, I would give him a different life. But there's nothing I can do to ease his grief."

"Sure there is," Scarlett said, looking surprised.

"What?"

"Go after him."

Like it was the most obvious thing. And maybe to her fearless, confident friend, it was. But Selena was different. She didn't think she could survive getting turned down again.

"He doesn't want me to go after him," she said. "He walked away. He said he couldn't be a father to this baby. He said he didn't love me."

Scarlett shook her head. "Because fear makes you stupid. And that's exactly what *he's* letting happen. But you're letting him hide. You're letting him give in to it. Don't let him. Or at least make him tell you no again. Come on, Selena. He can be a coward all he wants, but you're not a coward. Make him look you in the eye in the light of day and say he doesn't want you or the baby. Make him tell you he doesn't love you. And then make him tell you he's not just saying no because he's afraid."

Selena's heart thundered faster. It hadn't even occurred to her that it might not be over. That there might be something she could do to fix this. "But if he rejects me…"

"Then he rejects you." Scarlett shrugged, looking pragmatic about it.

Selena closed her eyes. "I never wanted to be that

woman. That woman who was such a fool over a man. My mother... She stayed with my father even though he was awful. Even after she left him, she missed him. The man who abused her, Scarlett—she said she missed him. I just don't... I don't want to be that person."

Scarlett frowned. "I can understand that. Really. But you know, hopefully, if you go make a fool of yourself for him, he'll make a fool of himself for you at some point, too. If you're going to be together for your whole lives, then there should be a lot of chances for both of you to chase each other down. For both of you to be idiots over love. I guess that's the big difference, right? Your mother was the one doing all of the giving, and your father did all of the taking."

Selena bit her lip. "It would never be like that with Knox."

"Well, there you go," Scarlett said, extending her arm out wide. "It's not the same."

Selena shook her head and sighed deeply. "No. I guess it's not." She put her hand on her stomach. "I don't feel in any way emotionally prepared for this."

"Well, good," Scarlett said, laughing. "Because if you did, I would have to break it to you that you're actually not. It would be up to me to tell you that you are in no way prepared. No matter what you might think."

"It's that different?"

Scarlett nodded. "Harder. Better, too."

Like love in general, Selena supposed.

She stood up, wobbling slightly, her balance off. She blamed the last few days.

"I have to go," Selena said.

"Where to?"

"I have to fly to Wyoming."

Thirteen

Knox had spent the rest of the day hungover and then had spent the next day working out on the ranch. Doing what he could to exhaust himself mentally and emotionally while he got all his thoughts together.

He had been pretty determined about what he wanted to do regarding Selena, but he had to be sure he was going to say the right thing. Because when you told a woman you didn't want her you had to prepare a pretty epic grovel.

He wasn't going to do anything to cause Selena more pain than he already had. And he had a lot of digging to do to find the right words. Through the dark and dusty places inside of himself.

He'd been restless and edgy in the house, and he'd decided to go out for a ride on the property. He urged his horse onward through the field, and he continued on to the edge of his favorite mountain. One with jagged rocks capped in snow that reached up toward the sky, like it was trying to touch heaven. Something he wished he could do often enough.

He wasn't a man who liked graveyards. But then, he supposed no one did. He just didn't find any peace in them. No, he found peace out here. With nature. That was when he felt closest with Ellie.

He looked around at the wildflowers that were blooming, little pops of purple and yellow against the green. Life. There was life all around him. A life to be lived. A life to enjoy. Maybe even a life to love, in spite of all the pain.

It was like that picture of Ellie. Sitting right here in this field surrounded by flowers.

He knew he wouldn't find her here, and yet he'd needed to come to this place. He'd avoided riding out here for the past two years.

Today had seemed like the day to go again. The last time he'd ridden out to this field, the last time he'd seen this view, he was a different man with a different future.

A man who'd known who he was and where he was going.

Now he was a man alone. Struggling to figure out what came next. If he could heal. If he wanted to heal.

An image of Selena flashed into his mind, of her hurt and heartbreak that night in the hotel room. She needed him. She needed him now.

Selena wasn't gone. Selena was here. And they could be together.

"I've got to figure out how to find some happiness, baby," he said, whispering the words into the silence. Whispering the words like a prayer. "I'm never going to forget you. I'm never going to stop loving you. But I'm going to learn how to love some other people, too. I'm going to take some steps forward. That doesn't mean leaving you behind. I promise."

He closed his eyes and waited, letting the silence close in around him. Letting himself just be still. Not working. Not struggling or fighting. Just existing. In the moment and with all the pain that moment carried.

The breeze swirled around him and he kept his eyes closed, smelling the flowers and the snow, crisp on the air as it blew down from the mountaintop.

That was assurance. Blessed assurance.

Letting go didn't mean forgetting. Moving forward wasn't leaving behind.

And in that moment, as he took a breath of the air that contained both the promise of spring and the bite of winter, he realized it was the same inside of him, too. That he could contain all of it. That he could hold on to that chill. That he could welcome the promise of new life.

There was room for all the love. For the bitter. For the sweet. For everything in between. There was no limit, as long as he didn't set it.

He knew what love could take away. He also knew what it could give. He had despaired of that for so long. That there were no mysteries left available to him. That he knew all about the heights of love and the lows of loss.

But he realized now that he had the most powerful love yet ahead.

The love he chose to give, in spite of the knowledge of the cost.

He just had to be brave enough to take hold of it.

He got down off his horse and bent to pick the brightest, boldest yellow wildflower. He held it between his thumb and forefinger. Ellie's flower. Just like in that picture. He stroked his thumb over one petal and a smile touched his lips.

He put the flower in his shirt pocket, just over his heart, and looked at the view all around him. A view he hadn't allowed himself to enjoy since he'd lost his daughter. A place that was full of good memories. Good memories he'd shut away so they couldn't hurt him.

But they were part of him. Part of his life. Part

of her life. And he wanted them. Wanted to be able to think of her and smile sometimes. Wanted to be able to remember the joy loving her had given him, not just the sorrow.

That was what he'd forgotten. How much joy came with love. Of course, you couldn't choose what you got. Couldn't take the good without risking the bad.

But you could choose love. And he was ready to do that.

It was time to walk forward. Into the known and the unknown.

And as long as Selena would have him, he had a feeling it was going to be okay.

He closed his eyes and faced the breeze again, let it kiss his face. Then he mounted the horse and took off at a gallop across the field, heading back toward the homestead.

He got his horse put away and strode out toward the front of the house. He needed to get his private plane fired up, because he had to get back to Texas, and he had to get back fast.

After what he had said to her, a phone call wasn't enough. He needed to go and find her. And he needed to tell her. To tell her he was sorry. To tell her they could do this. They could be together.

To tell her that he was done running.

There was something big, something fierce expanding in his chest. Something he hadn't felt in a long time.

Joy.

Selena.

And almost as if those feelings had brought her out of thin air, he looked up when he reached the front of his house and there she was. Standing in the center of the driveway, looking small and pale and a little bit lost. Selena Jacobs didn't do lost, and he had a feeling he was the cause of that desolate look on her face.

His heart clenched tight, guilt and love pouring through him.

"What are you doing here?" he asked.

She lifted her chin. "I came to get you."

"You can't be here to get me. I was about to get on a plane to go get *you.*"

Her bottom lip wobbled. "What?"

"I don't know what you're here for, Selena. But you have to hear me out first. Because I have to tell you. I have to tell you about everything I've realized. It's been a hell of a time."

"Yeah," she said, her tone dry. "You're telling me."

"I'm sorry," he said. "I'm sorry that I hurt both of us, but most especially you. I'm sorry that I did so much damage. I was afraid to move on. Because… because of the guilt. I just… The guilt and the fear. It isn't that I don't want the baby. It isn't that I don't love you. I do. I want you, and our baby, so much I ache with it. I want so much that it scares me, Selena, because I haven't wanted a damn thing in years. I haven't let myself want anything. Not even food. Because wanting, needing, *loving*, in my experience has meant devastation. I can't come up with another excuse. It's just that. I am so afraid that I might lose you someday. That if I love you too much, want to hold you too close, that something will happen, and I'll have to face that dark tunnel again. I couldn't survive it, baby. I couldn't. You've meant everything to me for a long time. And now, wanting you as a lover, loving you as a woman, I know that the loss of you would destroy me. The loss of our life. The loss of our child…

"But I can't live that way. I can't live in fear. I can't live holding on to only bad feelings to try and protect myself."

He walked toward her, took her hands. "I called Cassandra. Drunk off my ass. She said something to me… She was right. She said you have to love the person you find more than you love your life together. What Cassandra and I had felt perfect. But only as long as it *was* perfect. Once that fractured, we couldn't put it back together. We didn't want to. We loved what we had more than we loved each other. But when I fell in love with you, Selena, we had nothing. Nothing but those broken pieces. And what you said… I think it's the way forward. That we put these broken pieces together and we make something new. I can't go back. I can never be who I was. But I can try to be something new. To be something different. I can try to be the man you deserve."

She said nothing. Instead she sobbed as she threw her arms around his neck and clung to him, her tears soaking into his shirt. "Seriously?" she asked, the word watery.

"What seriously?"

"You really want to do this?"

"I need to," he said. "I need you. I realized something today, walking around the property. Winter and spring exist side by side here. It's been winter inside of me for a long time. And there's a part of me that's afraid of what letting go of that means. That it means I don't love Ellie enough. Or that I didn't."

"Of course you loved her enough," Selena said. "Of course you do. I know that in our lives together I want to honor that. This baby, this child, is never going to replace what you lost."

"I know," he said. "That was what I realized. I can make room in my heart for both of them." He reached into his pocket and removed the yellow flower, holding it out for her. "This is us. This spring. New life. A new season. I want to make room inside of me for that. I want less cold. Less fear. More of this."

"Please," she said, smiling and taking the flower

from his hand. "Yes, please. More spring. A lot more."

"I love you," he said. "I love you knowing that love is the most powerful thing on earth. That having it makes everything brighter, that losing it can destroy your whole world. I love you knowing what it might cost. And maybe that's a strange declaration, but it's the most powerful one I've got."

He cupped her chin, lifted her face to meet his. "When you're young, you get to dive into things headlong. You get to embrace those big, scary feelings not knowing what might wait for you on the other side. I know. But I want to choose a life with you. More than anything, I want to love you. If you want to love me." He let out a long, slow breath. "You know, if you still can love me."

"I do love you," she said. She held on to his face, met his eyes. "I love you so much, Knox. And the thing is, I could never tumble headlong into it when I was younger because I was scared. But I've grown up. I trust you. And trust has always been the key. I know what kind of man you are. I was afraid of love for a long time, but I was never afraid of you."

"But I hurt you."

"Yes," she said. "You did. But you were hurting, too. You didn't hurt me because you were a bully or because you enjoyed causing me pain. You did it because you were running scared. I get that. But that doesn't mean I'm not going to make you pay for it later."

"Oh, are you?"

"I am." She smiled. "I'm going to make you give my skin-care line preferential shelving in your supermarkets."

"Corporate blackmail."

"Yes," she said, "corporate blackmail. But it could be worse. It could be sexual blackmail."

He wrapped his arm around her waist and drew her up against his body. "Honey," he said, "you couldn't stick to sexual blackmail."

"I sure as hell could," she said, wiggling her hips against him. "And you would suffer."

He leaned forward and nipped her lower lip. "You would suffer."

"Okay," she said, her cheeks turning pink. "Maybe I would."

"Will you marry me, Selena? Marry me and make a new life with me? I'll never be the man that I was. But I hope the man I am now is the one for you."

Her smile turned soft. "He is. Believe me," she said, "he is."

"So that's a yes?"

"Yes," she said. "I never thought I would walk down the aisle for real. But, Knox, if ever I was going to, it had to be with you."

He looked down at Selena, at the woman he had

known for so many years, the woman he'd gone on such a long journey to be with.

"Right now," he said, "this moment... It can only ever be you. You're the one worth being brave for. You're the one who made me want to start a new life. And I'm so damned glad that you did."

"Me, too," she said and then squeaked when he picked her up off the ground and held her to his chest.

"I'm also glad that you saved me a flight," he said, heading back toward the house with her in his arms.

"Well, I'm glad to be so convenient."

"You're more than convenient," he said. "You're inconvenient. You made me change. Nobody likes that."

"Oh dear," she said, "however will you punish me?"

He smiled. "I'll think of something."

"You've always been my best friend," she said, hours later when they were lying in bed together, thoroughly sated by the previous hour's activities. "And now you're more. Now you're everything."

"I'm happy to be your everything, Selena Jacobs. I'm damned happy that you're mine."

He kissed her, a kiss full of promise. A kiss full of hope for the future.

And he smiled, so happy that for the first time in an awfully long time he had both of those things. And more important, he had love.

Epilogue

A child's laughter floated on the wind, and Selena ran to keep up with the little figure running ahead of her. She had long, dark hair like her mother, and it was currently bouncing with each stride.

She had her father's eyes.

Selena's husband was lingering behind her, his speed slowed by the fact he was holding their new son.

Selena turned to look at them both. Knox was clutching the five-month-old baby to his chest, his large hand cradling the downy head. Knox was such a good father.

He was caring, and he was concerned, and he had

a tendency to want to rush to the doctor at the very first sniffle, but she couldn't blame him. And watching the ways in which their children had opened him up...it made her heart expand until she couldn't breathe.

"Carmela!" Selena shouted. "Slow down."

Their daughter stopped and turned to look at them, an impish grin on her three-year-old face. She stopped, in the field of yellow-and-purple flowers, with the snow-covered mountains high and imposing behind her.

Selena turned back and saw that Knox had stopped walking. That he was just standing there, staring at Carmela.

Selena took two steps back toward him and put her hand on his forearm. "Are you okay? Do you need me to take Alejandro?"

"No," he said, his voice rough.

Carmela was turning in a circle, spinning, careless and free out in the open.

Knox couldn't take his eyes off her. He was frozen, his expression full of awe.

"What is it?" Selena asked.

"I just can't believe it," he responded. "That I have this again. This chance to love again. To love her. To love him." He brushed his hand over baby Alejandro's head. And then he turned those gray eyes to her. His desire for her was hot, open. It made her shiver. "To love you."

He leaned in and kissed her, and she shivered down to her toes.

"I remember feeling like I had nothing," he said. "Nothing to hope for. Nothing to hold. And now…I have hope. I have a future. And my arms are full."

Selena wrapped her arms around him and rested her head on his chest. "My best friend knocked me up on accident," she said. "And all I got was…this whole wonderful life."

He kissed her one more time, and when they parted she was breathless. Then the two of them walked on toward their daughter, toward the future. Together.

* * * * *

Don't miss a single installment of the
TEXAS CATTLEMAN'S CLUB: THE IMPOSTER.
*Will the scandal of the century lead to love for
these rich ranchers?*

THE RANCHER'S BABY
by New York Times *bestselling author
Maisey Yates.*
RICH RANCHER'S REDEMPTION
by USA TODAY *bestselling author
Maureen Child.*
A CONVENIENT TEXAS WEDDING
by Sheri WhiteFeather.
EXPECTING A SCANDAL by Joanne Rock.
REUNITED...WITH BABY
by USA TODAY *bestselling author Sara Orwig.*
THE NANNY PROPOSAL by Joss Wood.
SECRET TWINS FOR THE TEXAN
by Karen Booth.
LONE STAR SECRETS by Cat Schield.

*If you're on Twitter, tell us what you think of
Harlequin Desire! #harlequindesire*

Get 2 Free Books, Plus 2 Free Gifts—

just for trying the Reader Service!

HARLEQUIN *Desire*

HD17R3

*Billionaire Broderick Steele was raised to hate his rival,
Glenna Mikkelson-Powers—even if she's the sexiest woman he's
ever known. Then, amid corporate mergers and scandal, they
find an abandoned baby who could be Broderick's...or Glenna's.
Playing house has never been so high stakes!*

Read on for a sneak peek of
THE BABY CLAIM
by USA TODAY bestselling author Catherine Mann,
the first book in the *ALASKAN OIL BARONS* saga!

Being so close to this man had never been a wise idea.

The sensual draw was too strong for any woman to resist for
long and stay sane. Broderick's long wool duster over his suit was
pure Hugo Boss. But the cowboy hat and leather boots had a hint of
wear that only increased his appeal. His dark hair, which attested to
his quarter-Inuit heritage, showed the first signs of premature gray.
His charisma and strength were as vast as the Alaskan tundra they
both called home.

In a state this large, there should have been enough space for
both of them. Theoretically, they should never have to cross paths.
But their feuding families' constant battle over dominance of the
oil industry kept Glenna Mikkelson-Powers and Broderick Steele
in each other's social circles.

Too often for her peace of mind.

Even so, he'd never shown up at her office before.

Light caught the mischief in his eyes, bringing out whiskey
tones in the dark depths. His full lips pulled upward in a haughty
smile.

"You're being highly unprofessional." She narrowed her own
eyes, angry at her reaction to him as she drank in his familiar
arrogance.

Their gazes held and the air crackled. She remembered the feeling all too well from their *Romeo and Juliet* fling in college.

Doomed from the start.

He was her rival. His mesmerizing eyes and broody disposition would not distract her.

She jabbed a manicured finger in his direction. "Your father is up to something."

She scooped up a brass paperweight in the shape of a bear that had belonged to her father. Shifting it from hand to hand was an oddly comforting ritual. Or perhaps not so odd. When she was a small girl, her father had told her the statue gave people power, attributing his success to the brass bear. After the last year of loss, Glenna needed every ounce of luck and power she could get.

"There's no need to threaten me with your version of brass knuckles." Humor left his face and his expression became all business. "But since you're as bemused by what's happening as I am, come with me to speak to your mother."

"Of course. Let's do that. We'll have this sorted out in no time." The sooner the better.

She wanted Broderick Steele out of her office and not a simple touch away.

Don't miss
THE BABY CLAIM
by USA TODAY *bestselling author Catherine Mann,*
the first book in the **ALASKAN OIL BARONS** *saga!*
Available February 2018
wherever Harlequin® Desire books and ebooks are sold.

And then follow the continuing story of two merging oil families competing to win in business...and in love—

THE DOUBLE DEAL
Available March 2018

THE LOVE CHILD
Available April 2018

THE TWIN BIRTHRIGHT
Available May 2018

www.Harlequin.com

Want to give in to temptation with
steamy tales of irresistible desire?

Check out **Harlequin® Presents®,
Harlequin® Desire** and
Harlequin® Kimani™ Romance books!

New books available every month!

CONNECT WITH US AT:

Harlequin.com/Community

 Facebook.com/HarlequinBooks

 Twitter.com/HarlequinBooks

 Instagram.com/HarlequinBooks

 Pinterest.com/HarlequinBooks

ReaderService.com

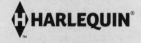 **HARLEQUIN®**

**ROMANCE WHEN
YOU NEED IT**

PGENRE2017

When it comes to sweet and sexy romance,
no one does it like *New York Times*
bestselling author

MAISEY YATES

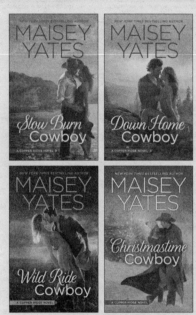

*Come home to Copper Ridge, where sexy cowboys
and breathtaking kisses are just around the corner!*

Order your copies now!

HQN™

www.HQNBooks.com

Reward the book lover in you!

Earn points from all your Harlequin book purchases from wherever you shop.

Turn your points into *FREE BOOKS* of your choice
OR
EXCLUSIVE GIFTS from your favorite authors or series.

Join for FREE today at
www.HarlequinMyRewards.com.

Harlequin My Rewards is a free program (no fees) without any commitments or obligations.

MYR17